D1488846

DIVINE INTERVENTION

ORLANDO A. SANCHEZ

BITTEN PEACHES
PUBLISHING

ABOUT THE STORY

How do you stop a god? Monty and Simon don't know, but they better find out...fast.

The NYTF Command Hub has been destroyed, the Director is in critical condition, and a cryptic message has been left for the Montague and Strong Detective Agency... in blood.

When Monty and Simon discover Mahnes, a Soul Renderer and Dark Mage, is behind the attack, they realize they are outclassed and outgunned. Something or someone is controlling Mahnes and they need help.

Now Monty and Simon must face an ancient god, one they thought they had defeated and banished.

They were wrong.

QUOTATION

I became insane with long intervals of terrible sanity.

-Edgar Allen Poe

Do not go gentle into that good night,
Old age should burn and rave at close of day;
Rage, rage against the dying of the light.
-Dylan Thomas

ONE

By the third hour of agony, I was convinced he was trying to kill me.

I saw the runes pulse slowly on the wooden floor. The entire room radiated power and simultaneously dampened it. The floor of the windowless space was Australian Buloke, with the walls and ceiling being some kind of reinforced steel.

It felt like standing in some kind of hi-tech mage cell. Around us sat several racks with assorted weights, some conventional and some not. One corner held an old 454 engine block for a '91 Chevy SS, attached to a complicated pulley system. Next to it, sat a pair of two hundred-pound dumbbells.

Part of me wanted to scoff and say this was just Hammertime showing off, but I knew she was strong—I just hadn't realized she was "use an engine block for exercise" strong.

Off to the side, away from the center of the floor, stood Monty, sipping from his cup of tea, and Ursula, Lead

Director of the DAMNED and owner of the space we were currently occupying. A little distance from them both lay my hellhound, languidly taking in the scene of my destruction.

I refocused on the thin old man standing in front of me. He radiated a deep undercurrent of power, even in this space. His close-cropped hair seemed to glow, a white crown glimmering in the subtle light of the training room. His eyes were still the same: deep, dark pools of emptiness.

Impossible to read.

"Again," the old man said, tapping his short staff on the smooth wooden floor. "Repeat the technique. Attack."

I hesitated. He didn't know what he was asking me to do.

"I don't think this is a good idea," I said. "I don't have a setting on this thing. It's either a full blast of destruction or nothing. There's no in-between."

Master Yat narrowed his eyes at me. Easily a three on the glare-o-meter, and if I had to guess, he wasn't even trying.

"That"—he pointed his staff at me to make his point —"is your problem. You lack self-control. What you need is a degree of modulation."

"Modulation? As in blasting only half this place apart instead of blowing the entire building into rubble?"

"Do *not* blow my building into rubble," Ursula, our host, grumbled. "I deal with your destruction on a regular basis. I will not have my HQ reduced to a crater."

"Simon," Yat said with a small sigh, "nuance is your friend. The energy you are wielding requires awareness and subtlety. If you fail to control it, it *will* control...and over-come...you."

"Subtlety?" Ursula scoffed. "These three are as subtle as a charge of already detonated C4. You're wasting your time, Master Yat."

"My middle name *is* subtlety," I said, mocking offense. "I know when to unleash the devastation and when to hold back. Besides, I'm not the one tearing the city apart."

Ursula walked over to a counter and picked up a folder, holding it up to me.

"Know what this is?" she asked. "I'll give you one guess."

"No idea. A list of the latest bear sightings in the city?"

"Oh, the humor, I can barely contain myself," she replied with a glare. "No. This is an action report from where I spent my evenings for the last few days."

"The local forest? Where do bears go at night? Do you have a cave somewhere?"

"No," she said with a tight smile, "this bear has been spending her nights in Queens. Do you know why?"

"Lots of trees?" I asked, shrugging my shoulders. "I heard bears love trees."

She glared at me, and I knew where this was going.

"It would seem..." She opened the folder and began reading. "At least according to the engineers on site, that the Unisphere suffered a catastrophic failure of its pedestal, resulting in the entire structure rolling down the park and into"—she peered closer at the report—"the Arthur Ashe Tennis Stadium. Causing extensive damage to both."

I glanced over at Monty, who was conveniently sipping his tea and hiding his face.

"Sounds serious," I said. "Any idea how something like that could happen?"

"You mean barring an earthquake?" Ursula looked from Monty to me. "I guess it would require an immense release of uncontrolled power to destroy that pedestal. Any idea how *that* could happen?"

"None," I said, shaking my head slowly. "I barely visit Queens these days. Busy with cases and such."

"Funny you should say that," she said, reaching into the folder and pulling out several sheets of paper and handing them to me. "These are from some of the surveillance cameras in the area. We keep close tabs on beings of power residing in the city...even in Queens."

"Do you, now?" I said, looking down at the sheets of paper. "Imagine that."

I was looking down at grainy surveillance time-stamped photos of Monty, my hellhound, and me meeting the Archive Guard, with the Unisphere in the background.

"From what I can see, the Unisphere is still intact in these photos," I said, handing her back the photos. "Not seeing your point."

"Oh, I'm sorry," she said, handing me another set of time-stamped photos. "I meant to show you *these*."

The second set of photos showed Monty, my hell-hound, and me with the Unisphere in the distance...rolling at us. The next photo showed the devastating impact of the Unisphere into the tennis stadium. The damage was massive.

"That wasn't us," I said, shaking my head again as I handed back the photos. "You really think we possess that much power? I'm flattered, really, but there are other beings in the city that could pull that off, you know."

"*They* weren't visiting the Auer that day, *you* were. Like I said, you three are about as subtle as a brick to the face."

The insinuation angered me, because we were quickly becoming the default destroyers of the city. If something exploded, imploded, or was obliterated, then it had to be the Montague and Strong Detective Agency.

Frankly, it was getting on my nerves. The problem was that, this time, she wasn't too far off the mark. We weren't directly responsible, but I could see how it could look like we were.

"It wasn't us," I said, letting an edge creep into my voice. "Drop it."

"Not happening," Ursula said, matching the menace in my voice. "This is what *I* have to do when you three are being *subtle*."

"At least I don't go around with a Mjolnir knockoff, Hammertime," I snapped. "I don't see you trying to harness insane amounts of energy. What do you do? Form your Hammer of Doom and swing away? Sounds real discreet."

"Simon," Monty warned before turning to Ursula. "Apologies. It would appear he has suffered several head injuries from the training."

"No need," Ursula growled, staring at me. "You think what you're doing here is so hard? You need to get your power under control."

"I'm the only one imitating a punching bag on this floor while you and Monty just spectate. So, yes. It's not as easy as I make it look."

Peaches gave me a low rumble from the side of the floor.

<Don't make the bear lady angry. She gave me good meat.>

<Glad your meat is more important than your bondmate being insulted.>

<She didn't insult you. You're not listening to the old stick man. Try harder.>

<Try harder?>

<Are your ears broken? Yes, try harder.>

Even my hellhound was giving me attitude...incredible.

"Focus," Yat said, getting my attention. "Ursula was gracious enough to provide us with a null training area. We *will* honor her gesture, yes?"

"Yes," I said, properly chastised. "Sorry, Hammertime, no offense."

She must have felt bad for me, because she let me get away with the nickname with only a glare.

"Keep calling me that and I will show you what my hammer can do."

I stood corrected and graced her with a smile, which vanished as Yat's short staff delicately tapped me in the head with a loud *thwack*.

Ursula burst into laughter and Monty conveniently happened to look away as a fit of coughs overcame him.

"I said focus," Yat said, placing the tip of the staff on the floor again. "What you need is nuance."

"Nuance? Oh, is that what we've been working on for the last three hours? Nuance?"

"No," Yat said with a small smile. "I have been using overwhelming force and pain. It seems to be the only language you understand when it comes to training."

He glanced at Ursula and motioned for her to come to the center of the floor.

"I'm not fighting a bear," I said, shaking my head slowly. "With or without a hammer."

"It wouldn't be much of a fight, trust me," Ursula said, focusing on Yat and giving him a short bow.

"Please create your hammer," Yat said softly. "Here"—he pointed to a spot on the floor with his staff—"on this location."

Ursula extended a hand and focused. A swirl of orange and silver energy flowed from her hand and coalesced on the floor where Yat indicated, creating her hammer. It was a massive, rune-covered weapon.

It may not have been Mjolnir, but Monty told me it did belong to the Finnish god of thunder and storms. Ursula never shared how she managed to get hold of it, but now that I was able to see it up close, the last thing I wanted was for her to swing that thing in my direction.

"Nice hammer. Must be great for those DIY projects around the home," I said, then looked at Yat. "So she can form her hammer? She must have done that thousands of times. It can't be that difficult for her."

Yat nodded.

"Please form your blade, Simon," Yat said. "As you say, it's not very difficult."

I focused my energy and created the silver mist that would become Ebonsoul. I let it race around my arm and form near my hand—and then it evaporated.

Ursula gave a small chuckle.

"What's the matter? Having trouble making that mist firm?"

"Ursula," Yat said, shaking his head. "Don't distract him."

"Apologies, Master Yat," Ursula replied, then looked at me. "You're standing in the DAMNED HQ, rocket scientist. Do you even know what DAMNED stands for?"

"Disturbed And Mutant Nulls—Extremely Dense?"

"Is that what passes for wit with you?" Ursula turned to Monty. "How do you deal with him?"

"In small doses, usually," Monty said. "Most of the time, I ignore him."

"The one part you got right was 'nulls,'" Ursula said, turning back to me. "This entire building is a null zone, Einstein. One of the strongest in the entire city."

"Wait," I said, the realization dawning on me. "How did you form your hammer, then?"

"Now, you're beginning to get it," Ursula said with a wide grin. "Some of us are just skilled, and others"—she reabsorbed her hammer into her hand—"have to learn the hard way: like you. Master Yat, do you still require my presence? It's been a long night. I'd like to get some sleep before morning."

"No, *Daxiong*," Yat said, with a slight bow. "Thank you again for the use of your training space."

Ursula returned the bow and left the training space.

"If this is a null space, how did she manage to do that?"

"Nuance," Yat said, tapping the floor again. "Now, attack."

"Right," I said, still concerned. "I don't want to hurt you."

"You are welcome to try, but your efforts have been somewhat lacking," Yat replied, stepping back into a relaxed pose. "Are you not feeling sufficiently motivated?"

"No—I mean, yes!" I quickly corrected. "My motivation is off-the-charts right now."

"Ah, good. Then attack...and this time, make me understand that you pose a real threat."

TWO

"You expect me to form my blade?"

"I expect you to present a real threat. Form your blade or use your ability, if you can."

I felt the power within and around me. That wasn't the issue. Accessing that power was the hard part. It felt like trying to grab smoke. Ursula wasn't kidding when she said the null zone was strong.

"How am I supposed to do that?" I asked, tired and frustrated. "This place is designed to stop me from doing exactly what you want me to do."

"Which makes it the perfect place to train," Yat said with a small smile that only irritated me further. "Do you think your enemies will stand idly by, providing you the luxury of doing whatever you want to do whenever you want to?"

"No. My enemies are usually the more on the 'obliterate to dust' side of the equation. If I can't access my power, things get lethal in a hurry. Good thing Monty is usually there in those situations."

"Except when he isn't," Yat said. "What if you are alone? No Tristan, no hellhound. Then what?"

"Then discretion is the better part of valor and I employ my ultimate move—run like hell."

"And if you can't run? If Tristan is hurt and you must, as a shield-warrior, protect him or your hellhound? Would you abandon them?"

"Not while I'm still breathing."

Yat nodded.

"Ursula formed her hammer in this place." Yat turned to look at Monty. "Can you cast?"

Monty formed an orb of bright white energy in response.

"Show off," I said, glaring at Monty before turning back to Yat. "So, basically what you're saying is that I'm the slow one in the class?"

"Yes and no. You're not a mage, but you are trying to act like one."

"I don't understand," I said, confused. "Are you trying to say I want to go around destroying everything in sight?"

"Not all mages have a propensity for destruction." Yat glanced at Monty. "Just some battlemages I know."

"Me too. What exactly do you mean, then?"

"You sense the energy around and within, yes?"

I nodded.

"It's all around me. Accessing it is the problem."

"There are mages, sorcerers, and wizards," Yat said. "These are generalities, not specific distinctions."

"Have you ever tried to call a mage a wizard? They get specifically pissed off immediately."

"Mages, sorcerers, and wizards all manipulate energy," Yat continued, ignoring me. "They do this in various ways using distinct methods, but it is still energy manipulation."

"You're not a mage," I said. "How do you do what you do? I've never seen you do finger-wiggles."

"Correct. I step into the flow of energy and adjust its direction."

"That sounds like something Rey—you don't know him —told me a while back. Mages store energy in their bodies, but I need to tap into the energy around me, like the Force?"

"It is not tapping into the Force," Yat corrected with a small sigh. "It is becoming one with the energy around you."

"You mean more like I'm one with the Force and the Force is with me?"

Another blur and Yat's staff introduced me to immediate pain across my ribs.

"Do you mean 'the Force' like that?"

"How am I supposed to tap into the energy around me when I'm in agony?" I said, rubbing my ribs. "Sounds counterproductive."

Monty gave me a glare and shook his head.

"Would you prefer I have you carry me everywhere while you train?" Yat said with a slight smile. "Would that be easier for you, help you focus?"

"What? No. What are you talking about? How is that going to make it easier to tap into the energy around me?"

"Easier for me to tap into your forehead with my staff. Maybe loosen some of the rocks in there."

"Can we stop with the tapping? No tapping."

"Exactly. Not tap into, align with," Yat said, pointing at me with his staff, which was dangerously close to my head.

"It is easier to move a boulder if you are pushing it in the direction it is already going. You move with the energy, not against it."

"That sounds ideal; except, how do I even discover the flow to align with it? I can sense it, but that doesn't mean I know which direction it's going. With me, most of the time it's spray and pray. Not exactly the best strategy."

"Not at all, which is why we are in this space. There is energy all around you. In order to access it, you must discern the flow, not just feel it."

"Oh, is that all?" I asked. "Well, now I'm set. *Discern,* not just feel. Totally clear now."

I didn't even see the staff move this time before it *thwacked* me across the side of the head.

"If you had to learn under my teacher, we would have had to bury you several times over for your responses alone," Yat said as I rubbed the side of my head. "Less talking, more listening."

"Ow," I said. "I actually felt that you know. Immortal doesn't mean impervious to pain."

"I know. Now, focus: how will you face those who would prevent you from accessing your power?"

"By discerning the flow?"

"Precisely," Yat said with a nod, gesturing around him with an arm. "Now, how will you do it in this environment?"

I narrowed my eyes and saw the runes all around the space.

"I can see the runes, I just don't see a flow or any way around them."

"In order to find the flow, you must find a way to work

around the obstacles. The runes in this place are a series of obstacles designed to stop the use of energy."

"I just said that," I replied frustrated. "The runes are stopping me."

"No, they are merely in your way. You are stopping yourself," Yat said, extending his arm, flinging his staff away from his body. It hovered in the air several feet away. "You must find the way around the obstacles. Stop trying to be a mage."

"You may not be a mage, but you really sound like one," I said, glancing at the floating staff. "Right, I need to find my way around the runic defenses."

"Now you are beginning to understand."

"Do you have a map?"

"I do," Yat said. "I will help you see it."

He extended his arm again and the staff flew into his hand.

"That doesn't look like help," I said warily. "That looks more like you're about to unleash the pain."

"I have found that pain is one of the purest forms of motivation," Yat said. "Especially when confronted with obscurity. It provides clarity of vision. This will help you see the flow."

"Clarity of vision? We have different definitions of pain, I think."

"Stop thinking and do."

He lunged forward and attacked.

To say Master Yat was fast would be a ridiculous understatement.

His staff peppered me with blows three times in the chest before I could register he was on me. The pain blossomed in my torso as he swept the staff back and around in a downward arc.

It caught one of my ankles, lifting my foot off the floor. I was momentarily horizontal as he proceeded to unleash a palm strike into my stomach, sending me into the wooden floor with force. I bounced with a grunt, rolling away as his staff slammed the floor a half second later with devastating power, missing me by inches.

I half hoped it would shatter, but no luck. Whatever it was made of was as strong as the Australian Buloke underneath us. I rolled to my feet, my body flushed with heat as it dealt with the damage. I needed to close the distance, but his staff kept me back.

"Do you feel the power around you?"

"Right now, I feel the pain *in* me," I said, dodging away. "Power, not so much."

"Still thinking," Yat said, sliding to the side and slashing horizontally, forcing me to duck. "Feel the energy around you."

"Hard to do when you're trying to smack me with your staff."

"The weapon is not the issue," he said, dropping the staff and closing the distance. "You talk too much. Less talk, more action."

He walked slowly toward me. Now I could engage him without his staff of pain and destruction. I closed the distance—and realized I had made a mistake.

A painful mistake.

I never knew what style Yat practiced. The one time I asked him, he had answered with, "Survival style," and proceeded to inflict pain. What I did know was that Yat was just as lethal without the staff as he was with it.

He met my advance with a barrage of punches. I managed to parry or block the first three. The remaining dozen or so broke through my defenses and impacted my upper body.

My ribs and kidneys were introduced to a percussive rhythm of pain as Yat proceeded to beat me like a drum. I managed to step back and unleash several fists of my own, but I was slow.

Too slow.

He grabbed my outstretched arm and turned into my body. Using my arm as a lever, he swung me over his hip and into the floor with force.

I groaned with pain as he released my arm and stepped back. I admired the ceiling for a few seconds as heat and pain rushed through my body.

"Are you feeling the force now?" Yat asked. "Or was that not the force you meant?"

"You actually have a sense of humor. Twisted, but still there," I said, getting unsteadily to my feet. "This isn't accomplishing anything. I'm exhausted and clearly outclassed. Unless you're teaching me how to be a punching bag. I don't need a special training session for that. I think I've mastered the art of pain absorption pretty well by now."

Yat bowed and turned to Monty.

"You and the hellhound need to leave, now," Yat said. It wasn't a request. "He needs to go further, and I fear you or his hound may reflexively try to protect him if either of you are present."

Monty bowed and patted Peaches on the head.

"We need to go," he said, creating a large sausage and feeding it to Peaches as he headed for the door. "He will be fine. Come now."

<The angry man says we need to go. Will the stick man hurt you?>

<Probably, but this is training. I'll be okay. Go with Monty. He made you delicious meat.>

<It is delicious. I will go with the angry man. If you need me to come back and bite the stick man, I will.>

<I don't recommend it. Go—I'll be fine. He's just going to make the training harder, that's all.>

I watched Monty and my hellhound leave the training area.

"You think you're at your limit," Yat said with his arms crossed behind him, examining me. "You are exhausted and can't possibly go on. Yes?"

"The thought has crossed my mind one or five times, yes," I confessed. "Can the rest of the training be theoretical? You know, we sit, you with some tea and me with a large mug of coffee, and discuss the intricacies of energy and its manipulation?"

Yat smiled.

That one gesture gripped me with more fear than any of his previous actions. It wasn't a smile of joy, or even of acceptance. It was an expression of lethal intent.

"The intricacies, as you call them, have been discussed," he said, pulling out two long rectangular objects from behind him. "Now, I will show you the application. You will do the same, or perish in the attempt."

"That's a little dark there," I said with a small chuckle. "I get the whole stern Master thing—I do, really—but perish? Seems excessive."

"Does it?" He flicked his wrists, and I realized he was holding two fans. "We will see."

I was about to comment something about not being that hot, but thanks for offering to keep me cool, when I got a better look at the fans he was holding.

These weren't normal fans.

They seemed to be made of lightweight black steel, each one about two feet in width fully opened. The edges looked razor sharp and I could see faintly glowing red runes on their surfaces.

"Those look sharp," I said, backing up. "Maybe put them away before someone gets hurt?"

"You want me to put them away?"

"Yes, that would be the best way to continue the training," I said drawing Grim Whisper. "With the fans put away."

He looked at Grim Whisper and graced me with another one of his chilling smiles.

"Do you plan on using that?"

"Only if you make me," I said, the fear very real in my voice. "You need to put those things away. Now."

"Make me," he said, closing the distance.

I raised Grim Whisper and fired.

THREE

A few things happened simultaneously.

Master Yat moved faster than before as he raised a fan and deflected my round, while using the other to slice through my mid-section.

I stumbled back in shock and pain as the wound in my midsection started bleeding. Heat flushed my body, but my wound was taking its time closing.

"You're complacent, Simon," Yat said, circling. "You think immortals can't die?"

"What kind of...what kind of fans are those?"

He flicked a fan up and let me see the runes inscribed on it.

"This should look familiar," Yat said. "You've seen these runes before, yes?"

"No," I said, distracted by the fact that I was still bleeding. "Never seen them before."

"Look again," he said calmly. "Look with your deeper sight."

There was something in his voice that made me focus

on the fan. I used my inner sight and focused on the runes. It took a few seconds before the realization hit me.

He nodded when he saw my expression, and it was in that moment that I truly and thoroughly understood: Master Yat had gone to the next level.

He was trying to kill me.

I had seen the runes on the fan before. They were the same runes I had seen on Evers' blade.

The Kamikira.

"Those runes..." I started. "How?"

"Now that you understand your situation, what will you do?" he asked, looking down at my slowly closing wound. "Besides bleed all over the floor?"

"Are you serious right now?" I demanded, raising my voice. "You're supposed to be helping me get a handle on this energy thing, not slicing me to ribbons."

"I *am* helping you," Yat said. "Access your power and stop me. Or die."

My choices were limited.

"Just for the record, those choices suck."

"Very often you will have to make the best of the choices you are given," Yat said. "Many times those choices will, as you say, *suck*."

It really came down to one choice—access my power. If I didn't, there was no way I could stop Yat or prevent my death. Not that I was certain I could, even if I had access to my power.

I blocked out the pain, the fact that my wound was barely healing, the heat threatening to barbecue me from the inside, and let my senses expand to the space around me.

Null runes were never arbitrary. I'd learned that from

watching Monty. The position and placement of each rune was intentional. Each one served a function, a purpose.

The runes in the DAMNED HQ were designed to stop active casting, rendering the space null, but Ursula was able to create her hammer and Monty managed an orb. Even Yat did his whole floating staff trick, which meant there was a workaround.

I had to find a passive way to activate my weapon, one that didn't trigger the nullifying effects of the runes around me.

I had managed to form Ebonsoul's mist, but somehow couldn't get it to solidify. I dodged back and grunted in pain as a fan narrowly missed my neck. Another fan sliced upward, forcing me to stumble back farther.

Yat spun around and dropped, slicing my outer thigh as I fired Grim Whisper again. He deflected the round as he sliced my arm, forcing me to drop my gun. Several more slashes followed as I backed up and removed my jacket.

"No weapons, no abilities. Only your wit and power can help you now," Yat said. "I could safely say that, in your current state, you are unarmed."

"Ouch," I said. "I almost felt that insult."

"Do you surrender?"

"Will you stop attacking me if I do?"

"No, it will only hasten your demise. I just wanted to know if you truly understood how pointless your resistance is in the face of overwhelming skill and power."

"Resistance is futile? Really?"

"In this case, yes. Accept the fact that I will cut your life short. It will make it easier for you."

"What is this, Master Yat-Villain Edition?" I asked. "You're supposed to be helping me train."

He waved a fan dismissively.

"What for?" he said. "It's clear you have resigned yourself to being a victim. How many times are you going to inform us that you are not a mage, and therefore we should extend special treatment to you?"

"Excuse me. It's..."

"Exhausting is what it is," Yat finished. "You fail to understand even the most rudimentary aspects of energy manipulation. This is not quantum mechanics, Simon."

"Sometimes it feels like it is."

"You are not making an effort. Even now, you use your words to deflect, stall, and to obscure."

"Obscure? I'm not trying to obscure anything."

"Not even honest with yourself," Yat said, shaking his head. "You hide your fear behind your words. What will you do when you encounter an enemy who will offer no hiding place? What then?"

"I have, and I'm still here."

"What happens when you are alone?" Yat said. "This is what you are not seeing. The time will come when it will just be you. No help, no backup—just you, your knowledge, and your power. What then?"

"I don't know," I said.

"Finally," Yat said with a brief nod. "An honest answer. Now, we can begin."

"Begin?"

Yat unleashed both fans at me as his staff flew back into his hand.

FOUR

Considering I wasn't going to master energy manipulation in the next two seconds, I calculated that the only way I could defend myself was to use a passive defense. Everything I had worked offensively. Grim Whisper's rounds could be deflected, and I couldn't form Ebonsoul, much less my unreliable Dawnward. Using a magic missile was out of the question, which only left one thing.

I reflexively pressed my mark and hoped it would work in a null zone.

The last time I had tried this I had been facing a homicidal Dex. I really hoped I hadn't broken my mark—not that meeting an annoyed Karma would be pleasant. If I could manage to step out of time without getting her attention, it would be the best of both worlds.

The design, an endless knot inscribed into the top of my hand, given to me courtesy of Kali, gave off a deep violet light which pulsed with energy. I looked around and saw trails of violet dancing in my vision.

Gradually, everything grew out of focus. So far so good.

That lasted all of half a second.

The heady smell of lotus blossoms and earth after a hard rain filled my lungs. This was followed by the sharp smell of cut oranges and an aroma hinting of cinnamon permeating the air.

"Shit," I muttered under my breath. "That's not good."

Time slowed and came to a pronounced and definitive standstill. I noticed Yat's lethal fans of death suspended in the air on their way to slice me to pieces as time crept to a visceral halt.

This sensation was similar to the time I was in Kali's temple. Rather than a sudden stop, time took its time slowing down to the point of stillness.

"Hello, Splinter," Karma said, appearing next to me and examining the fans headed my way. "Is this some new immortality-testing pasttime? Catching weapons?"

She was dressed in a basic black ensemble: black T-shirt, black jeans, and a pair of tall, lethal-looking Prada Lug-Sole leather combat boots, which easily added a few menacing inches of height to her stature.

On her hand, she wore an ornate silver ring that sported a stylized ruby B. Her hair was pulled back in a tight ponytail, which contained several small sharp-looking knives as accessories.

"I wasn't expecting you," I said quickly. "Last time I pressed my mark, nothing happened."

"You were facing Dexter Montague," she said, "in a different space. One he controlled. Not the easiest place to visit, even if I wanted to, which I didn't."

For the briefest of moments it sounded like she feared Dex. I was going to ask her, but I enjoyed breathing more than knowing whatever her answer would be. I couldn't imagine Karma, the agent of causality, being scared of anyone, but this was Dex. The Morrigan-dating mage Dex, who was just this side of insane—just.

Anything was possible.

"For the record, I didn't *summon* you," I said. "I'm trying to avoid those." I pointed at the twin fans of death headed my way. "The mark was the only thing I thought could work."

"Why?"

"Why did I think it could work, or why am I avoiding the fans?"

"Both."

"This place is a null zone."

"I'm aware," she said, giving me a look. "One of the strongest in the city."

"Active casting doesn't work, so I went for something passive. The mark and stepping out of time felt like the best option."

"Or you could just let the fans slice through you. You *are* immortal. It may sting, but you're in no danger of losing your life. A little pain is good for the soul."

"Yat just sliced me with one of them. The wound took longer than usual to heal," I said, showing her my midsection. "Not looking to enjoy that again."

She walked over to where the fans hung suspended in the air and nodded.

"Yat is full of surprises. I wonder where he located the runes to inscribe these," she said, touching a fan. "It certainly makes them dangerous."

"Dangerous? Those are the same runes I've seen on the kamikira blades I've faced."

"But they aren't kamikira *blades*, they're *fans*. The

runes make them decidedly more lethal, but these pose no fatal threat to you. They may cut, but they won't kill you, and whatever doesn't kill you...well you know the rest."

"I thought..."

"You *assumed* because they bore the same runes, that they were just as deadly," she said, turning to me. "A mistake like that could cost someone their life. Don't you think?"

"Shit. He lied to me?"

"Did Yat say they were deadly to you?"

"No," I said, thinking back to Yat's words. "He just said the runes would be familiar to me."

"He didn't lie to you," she said with a smile. "He planted the seed and you watered it. You formed a conclusion with insufficient information."

"Something like that, yes," I said. "Wait, you know Yat?"

"Splinter, I know *everyone*," she said, glancing at the frozen Yat. "Yat is an...*interesting* individual. You could stand to learn much from him. His methods are somewhat archaic, but they are effective."

"He thinks every lesson should have ample doses of pain."

"Like I said, effective," she said. "How do you intend to deal with him?"

"I need to neutralize the fans first, I think."

"Wrong—the fans are inconsequential. He is the primary threat. Do not let yourself be distracted. The staff he wields may not kill you, but it *will* break you."

"I don't know. I can't access my weapons; he neutralizes everything."

"Except this." She motioned around us with a hand. "You managed to buy yourself some time—literally."

"Wait, if the mark isn't affected by the null zone, does that mean stepping out of time neutralizes null zones?"

"Now you're beginning to ask the right questions," she said, snaking an arm around my shoulders, pulling me close and tapping my forehead with a manicured nail. "This mark Kali gave you is going to make you extremely popular in all the wrong circles. I love it."

"What do you mean?"

"You're coming along nicely," she said, ignoring my question. "Slowly, but masterpieces do take time." She glanced over at Yat. "I will tell you this: focus on the true threat."

"Could you be a little clearer?"

"No," she said with a smile and tapped my cheek with bone-jarring force. "I'm not here to *help* you, Splinter."

"Then why are you here?" I said, exasperated. "I mean, really, what is your purpose in my life?"

Karma nodded.

"Finally, some real questions. If you get to the answers, you will make your life easier and so much harder."

She disappeared a moment later.

"Typical karmic response," I muttered under my breath, looking around as I rubbed my cheek. I made sure to keep my voice low in case she was still nearby. "Would a simple answer kill you?"

I reached out to the energy within me and formed the silver mist that would become Ebonsoul. It enveloped my arm, forming the blade in my hand. It gleamed, the red runes pulsing slowly. I stepped up to the fans, carefully closing them as I walked past.

The aroma of wet earth and oranges dissipated as time snapped into its normal flow. Yat found Ebonsoul against his neck as his fans fell to the floor across the room.

"Yield," I said, applying pressure to Ebonsoul against his neck. "It's over."

"Well done," Yat said. "You utilized the one ability open to you. You only made two mistakes."

"I made no mistakes," I said smugly. "I have you dead to rights. You should surrender right now. It's over."

"As I was saying, you made two mistakes," Yat continued in his exasperating lecture voice. "Fatal errors, actually, had I been intent on ending your life."

"Not from where I'm standing."

"A situation I will rectify shortly."

"What? You're trapped. I have a live blade to your neck."

"One," he continued as if I wasn't holding Ebonsoul to his neck, "you left me with a weapon when you could have stripped it from my hands."

"You can't—"

In a rapid shift, he raised his staff between Ebonsoul and his neck, slamming the staff into my arm and loosening my grip.

I quickly tried to correct, but it was too late. He was too fast.

Yat ducked under my arm, jammed the staff into my knee, disrupting my balance while rotating away from me. I stumbled to the side. He buried his staff in my midsection, before driving a hammer fist into the side of my head. The room tilted on its axis for a second as stars danced in my vision.

An uppercut lifted me off my feet and sent me unceremoniously to the floor, again. The floor seesawed as I struggled to get to my feet. Another strike from the staff landed me on my back, gasping for air.

"Your second mistake was leaving an enemy alive when you held his life in your hands," he said, looking down at me. "From where *I'm* standing, you are now dead."

"You expected me to—"

The agony of the staff crashing into my head cut my words short as I lost consciousness.

FIVE

I opened my eyes and felt pain.

Everywhere.

A hazy figure entered my field of vision. It took me a few seconds to focus and even that small act hurt. I noticed I was still on the training floor of DAMNED HQ.

"The nightmare isn't over?" I said, squinting at Yat as he stared down at me. "Can I call a time out?"

I sat up slowly as my body screamed at me. Apparently my healing was slowed by the null effects of the room—something to remember if I ever found myself facing another lunatic with a staff claiming to be training me.

"I killed you," Yat said as I blinked against the pain. "Then, while you were dead, I killed everyone you loved and protected."

"Not a pleasant thought," I said, slowly sitting up. "How long have I been out?"

"A few minutes. Plenty of time to remove your head and eliminate your friends."

"Anyone ever tell you that your sense of humor is seriously twisted?"

"No one still living."

I stared at him for a few seconds. He had the kind of face that made it impossible to tell if he was joking. Based on my past experiences with him, he didn't even know the concept of a joke.

"I don't think you can eliminate *my* friends in a few minutes."

"I managed to dispatch *you* in a short time," he said. "Easily, I might add."

"After three-plus hours of getting me exhausted first."

"Do you think your enemies will allow you to rest between their attempts on your life?"

"My enemies aren't that considerate, no."

"Have you given thought to the next sequence of events following your death?"

"Not really how I start my day, Darth Yat."

"It bears thinking about," he said. "Every warrior must contemplate their death, especially you."

"Especially me? Because?"

"Your death would sever your bond with your hellhound. This, in turn, causes a cascade of destruction. Your hellhound would lose control, growing immensely. Tristan would then have to deal with that imminent threat, exposing himself to attack. He would be vulnerable to anyone with power—they both would be. It would take no more than a few minutes...for someone like me. You will face greater threats."

"How do you know this?" I said, surprised at his depth of knowledge about Peaches and my bond with him. "That's not exactly common knowledge."

Yat stepped closer to me and sat on the floor across from me. He did this effortlessly, folding his legs to make it seem that he had floated down to the floor. He extended his staff and pointed to my forehead.

I don't know if I was resigned to expecting his gentle *thwacks* of correction, or if the exhaustion I was feeling had finally won and taken over, but to my surprise, I managed to avoid flinching away from the weapon.

"This mark you now possess—what do you think it means?"

"Kali told me it would protect me, at least in the short term."

"And in the long term?"

"I'd have enemies looking to take out the 'Marked of Kali'. Powerful enemies."

"How do you face a powerful enemy, if your intent is to destroy them?"

Aware of the fact that his staff was still within striking distance, I decided to provide what I hoped would be a *thwack*-free answer.

"You study them first if you can, find their weaknesses, and exploit them. Use misdirection when you can, hiding your true intent until it is too late for them to defend against your final attack."

"That would work against a child," he said dismissively. "You are not facing children. Try again."

I focused through the fog of pain and exhaustion. My body was running hot trying to deal with the injuries, but it was taking its time.

"You defeat them without having to face them. You force them to defeat themselves. By the time you prepare an attack, it is simply to clean up. The battle is over."

Yat nodded.

"Now, how would you defeat an immortal detective, bonded to a hellhound, and befriended by a powerful mage?"

"I've never thought about how to defeat myself, Peaches, and Monty."

Thwack.

"Think about it now. How?"

"Turn our strengths into liabilities," I said, wary of another strike to my head. "Find out what makes us formidable and use it against us."

"How?"

"Poison Peaches. That removes one of our defenses," I said, the words difficult to complete. "Attack Roxanne at Haven—that would distract Monty enough to make him do anything to keep her safe."

"And you?" Yat asked softly. "What about the immortal?"

I shook my head.

"I don't know," I said, frustrated. "Serve me decaf? That would certainly take me out for a few hours."

Surprisingly, the next few seconds were *thwack*-free. I adjusted my position with a groan and looked at him defiantly while still aware that his staff was near my head. He stared at me pensively, before placing the staff across his lap.

"Tell me why your wound took so long to heal, and why you are wincing in pain even now."

"The null zone?"

"Correct," he said, extending a hand causing the fans to return to him. They disappeared from view a second later. "You thought it was the runes on my *shan*. You were wrong.

The fans are runed to make them lethal, yes, but they are not kamikira. They cannot kill you."

"So I heard. You led me to believe they were god-killers."

"I did no such thing," he said. "I merely reminded you of what the runes were. *You* believed them to be god-killers and acted accordingly."

"Misdirection," I said. "Show me one thing, but help me see something else entirely."

"Exactly. The human mind is easily deceived, especially from within. I merely helped you believe something you knew to be true: if kamikira are lethal, then a weapon bearing the same rune must be just as lethal."

"But that's not true, is it?"

"Of course not," he said. "If that were the case, kamikira weapons would overrun this plane. The process to make a kamikira blade has been lost to time. All that can be done now is to find the lost weapons imbued with the power of the original runes."

"But those runes you inscribed on the fans?"

"Only enhance my fans, not turn them into kamikira blades. To you, they are dangerous, not deadly. Stop stalling. How do you eliminate the immortal? How would you kill...you?"

"The null zone," I said as the realization hit me. "You create a null zone even more powerful than this one. Lure in the immortal, using his poisoned hellhound as bait while simultaneously attacking Haven. Divide and conquer. Once the immortal is in the null zone, you take him out with overwhelming force, too much for his body to heal."

"All of these situations have happened to you...independently," Yat said. "What will you do when they all occur at the same time?"

"When? Don't you mean if?"

"*When*, Marked of Kali," he said, getting to his feet. "If you can come up with this basic plan, do you really think it's beyond the machinations of those who would want you removed? Beings with minds infinitely more devious than yours?"

"Why would anyone want me removed?" I asked, slowly getting to my feet with another groan. "I mean, besides the multitude of entities we've managed to piss off and the assorted enemies we've collected recently."

"Before this mark, you were a nuisance, one that could be dismissed by beings much stronger than you. Now? Kali has announced to all who would listen"—he tapped my chest with a finger for emphasis—"that you are a threat that must be dealt with. And they are paying attention."

"I'll have to remember to thank her for that."

"Your time would be better invested learning to circumvent the properties of a null zone. It is almost certain you will be attacked this way. It is an efficient and powerful way to neutralize you. Tristan wields energy, and your hellhound is formidable, but you would pose the greatest threat."

"Me?" I said, not seeing it. "I don't understand. Both of them dwarf me in power. Have you seen what Peaches can do? Omega beams, planewalking, not to mention that sonic bark of his. Recently, he acquired a new skill, Hellfire: flame breath that can barbecue practically anything. As for Monty, he nearly went Archmage not too long ago with his schism, and you think *I'm* the major threat? I respectfully disagree."

"Yet, with all the power they both possess, they are mortal and can be killed. It may take some work, but it can be done. You, on the other hand, would prove difficult. If *I* were the one trying to eliminate this threat"—he tapped me in the chest with his staff—"I would start with *you*."

"That makes me feel all kinds of special," I said, realizing he was right. "How do I prevent that?"

"*Prevent* it? You don't. It is inevitable. The more you prepare and sweat in training—"

"The less you bleed on the battlefield," I finished. "I'd like to avoid any kind of bleeding anywhere, thank you."

"Then you *prepare*," Yat said. "You have the understanding. Now, you need to expand on it. Find a way to circumvent null zones. If you can step *out* of the flow of time, you can step *into* the flow of energy."

"I wish it were that easy."

"It is," Yat said. "All it takes is understanding and opportunity. I believe the latter approaches."

Ursula rushed into the training space, followed by Monty and Peaches.

"What happened?" I said, concerned, glancing at Peaches. "Whatever he chewed through, I'll replace it."

<I didn't chew through anything.>

<Sorry, boy, just being careful. She looks upset.>

<The bear lady gave me sausage. I chewed through that. It was good.>

<I'm sure it was. Let me find out why she looks unhappy.>

<She should eat more meat. Meat always makes me happy.>

"NYTF headquarters was attacked late last night," Ursula said, her voice grim. "A massive assault that obliterated one of the main buildings."

"That's called an occupational hazard," I said. "NYTF tangles with some nasty creatures. Part of the job."

"I'm aware," Ursula said. "Usually, this wouldn't even bear mentioning except for two things."

"Which are?"

"They usually confront the creatures they encounter, and this was a preemptive strike on their headquarters, which to my knowledge has never happened before."

"Wait a second. The NYTF doesn't have a 'headquarters,'" I said. "They have a series of locations throughout the city that act as hubs. It's safer that way, and harder to attack them."

"You're well informed for someone who isn't part of the Task Force," Ursula said. "No one really knows that."

"Angel—I mean, Director Ramirez is a close friend."

"That's the second reason. pne of my people on site says there's a message for the both of you."

"A message for us? Which location was hit?"

"Seward Park. The Director was on site during the attack. I don't think it was a coincidence."

"A preemptive strike while Ramirez was on-site? That sounds off."

"It sounds calculated."

The Seward Park Hub was located on the corner of Grand and Clinton streets. The block was dominated by Seward Park with several small businesses on the fringe of the property.

The NYTF had repurposed an old post office into one of their main hubs. From what I understood, it still operated as a post office. The NYTF had offices underground and on the second level of the building.

She let the words sink in for a few moments. The

reason for the multiple hubs was to make the Director of the NYTF a hard target. Ramirez had more enemies than anyone else I knew.

He stayed alive by being mobile. No one outside of his close circle of lieutenants knew where he would be on any given day, much less be able to plan an attack.

"What are you saying?"

"Someone knew he was going to be at the Seward Hub and chose that moment to unleash an attack that nearly killed him. He was betrayed."

"No...Where is Ramirez?"

"Critical at Haven," she said. "We need to go."

SIX

I turned to bow to Master Yat, but he was gone.

"Yat just Dark Knighted me," I said, looking around the training space, but he was nowhere to be seen. "How does he do that?"

"I don't try to explain Master Yat," Ursula said. "My life is complicated enough."

"Wait a minute, aren't you on DAMNED duty or something? Why are you coming with?"

"Do you know what it is I face on a regular basis to keep this city safe?" Ursula said, grabbing a bag and her jacket. "Do you know what the DAMNED do?"

"Not a clue," I said. "I know your group keeps nexus points safe, but I figured you guys were like glorified gatekeepers or caretakers of nexi. Or is it nexuses?"

"That's cute," Ursula said. "That's like saying your detective agency only *slightly* damages landmarks around my city while you go around detecting whatever it is you detect. Are you even a real detective?"

"For the record, it's my city too—and yes, I'm a real detective."

"We'll see, because this whole attack stinks," she said, pointing at me. "And somehow the two of you are involved."

"Excuse me?"

"They left you a message. One you need to see."

"Why not just tell me? It would make our lives easier."

"They weren't able to decipher it."

"But they know it's for us, how?"

"That part of the message was clear, it seems."

"Only part of the message was clear?"

"How about we go see and you can put those detecting skills of yours to use?" she said. "My people are solid. If they say there's a message for you, I believe them. Let's find out who would do this before you go around obliterating my city. The only good thing out of this is that it didn't happen on a nexus point."

"Then why are your people on site?"

"If you knew what we faced, I mean really knew, you wouldn't have to ask that question."

"Fine, what is it that you and the rest of the DAMNED face? Nexus smashers? Nexus catchers? Nexus monsters? What?"

"We face the Mourn."

"The morn? The nexus doesn't operate at night? What are these things?"

"M-O-U-R-N," Ursula spelled out for me. "Most nights it's Mournhounds, but there are worse things in the Mourn than the hounds."

"What do these hounds look like?"

"Think of the creature from *Alien*, only in the thousands, and eager to chew your face off." She glanced at Monty. "Especially if you wield runic energy."

"Those don't sound fun. Are you saying these morning-dogs attacked the NYTF HQ?"

"It's *Mournhounds,* and according to the survivors at the hub, it sounds like it, or something like them—which would be the worst possible development. *That* is why I'm coming with," she said. "I really hope it's not the case. The NYTF HQ is not on a nexus point, but anything is possible. Any more questions?"

"None," I said. "I'll meet you there."

"If you get there and see any shadowy, alien-looking creatures with more teeth than should be possible, do *not* engage them."

"I'm sure a few entropy rounds can take care of your hotdogs."

"*Mournhounds,* and entropy rounds are banned ordnance," Ursula replied. "How are you walking around with entropy rounds?"

"Did I say *entropy* rounds? I meant *Persuader* rounds. I get them mixed up all the time."

She narrowed her eyes at me and released a low growl. A Clint Glint with a growl was pretty impressive. I gave her a solid two on the glare-o-meter and bumped it up to three because of the growl.

"Let me say this in a way *you* can understand," she said, still glaring at me. "You are not to engage these creatures in any way—"

"I got it—"

"No, you don't," Ursula interrupted. "Both of you use runic energy. Admittedly I'm a little iffy about what powers your hellhound uses, but it's better to be safe than sorry. To the Mourn, a mage is the ultimate meal wrapped up in a convenient meat sac."

"And you say no one appreciates mages," I said, glancing at Monty. "I think the Mourndoggies would love you."

"She's serious," Monty said. "You should be, too. The Mourn are deadly to mages or any who use runic energy, which is why nulls have been tasked to the DAMNED."

"Fine," I said, raising a hand in surrender. "We will not engage anything suspicious until you and your hammer arrive on site."

"Excellent," she said, letting out a small sigh. "Last thing I need is to save your sorry ass."

Ursula headed out of the training space at a brisk pace. She took the stairs down to the garage where her car was stored.

"Did you hear that?" I said to Monty as we followed her down. "She called your ass sorry."

"I'm certain she was referring to you," Monty said as we reached the garage. "I strongly suggest you don't touch her car."

I took a moment to admire her auto. It was a black 1947 Plymouth Business Coupe and the gleaming wax coat was begging me to run my hand over the hood. I reached out to touch when Ursula growled again.

"What?" I said. "Just admiring the automotive art. Nice wax job."

"You want to keep that hand? Admire from a distance. The Widow doesn't like strangers, and neither of you are null. It might blast you into a wall, or worse," she said with a devious smile. "On second thought, if you really want to reach out and caress her, please, be my guest."

"You...are an evil bear," I said, pulling my hand away from the Widow. "Did Cecil rune this?"

"Yes. The Widow was designed specifically as a null siphon and was runed to deal with the damage the Mourn would throw at me," Ursula said, getting in and starting the engine with a roar. It settled into a throaty purr as the door to the garage opened. "Where's your ride? Or are you taking the mage express?"

"No mage express, thanks. We're right outside, to the left."

She glanced over and took in the Dark Goat.

"Sweet. You should let me drive it one day," she said as she slowly rolled out of the garage. "I love GOATs."

"I would, but it would probably be the last time you drove...anything ever," I said. "Cecil did a special number on the Dark Goat. One driver, period."

Ursula nodded.

"Sometimes I wonder about Cecil and SuNaTran," she said. "Meet you on site and remember what I said."

With a roar, Ursula and the Widow sped down the street.

SEVEN

There wasn't much left of the NYTF hub at Seward Park.

It looked like someone had used the building for RPG practice. I parked the Dark Goat behind the Widow, making sure the Dark Goat was locked after Peaches bounded out. As I got out and looked around, Peaches sniffed and chuffed, shaking his head.

<*This place smells bad.*>

<*Smells bad? How?*>

<*Very bad. It smells like the bad dogs.*>

<*Let me know if you see any of them.*>

"Peaches isn't enjoying the aroma of this place," I said under my breath as Monty and I surveyed the destruction, "says it smells bad."

"How bad? Can he tell what kind of creature was here?"

"Says it smells like Shadowhounds, but I don't remember them being this destructive. None of them were carrying rocket launchers the last time we crossed paths, at least not to my recollection."

"This wasn't the work of Shadowhounds."

"You know what did this?"

"I sincerely hope I'm wrong."

There were several groups examining what used to be the NYTF hub. Bright yellow caution tape cordoned off most of the area.

"Is this what a Mourn attack looks like?" I asked Monty, who was crouched near the ground next to me, examining what appeared to be gouges in the stone floor. "How did they manage this?"

"The Mourn would have no reason to attack the NYTF," Monty said. "The task force is comprised of sensitives, but not active users of energy. I have to agree with Ursula: This was an attack orchestrated to send a message."

"What message? 'We excel in death and carnage'?"

"Perhaps; it's possible it was a show of strength."

"I'm liking this message less by the second," I said. "Why go through all of this to send a message?"

"Obliterating this hub was done for two reasons," Monty said, standing and brushing off his sleeves. "To get our attention, and to be taken seriously."

"Whoever did this seriously has my attention."

Outside the cordon, I saw a group of EMTe buses loading those who still had a slim hope. I looked around for Frank, but didn't see him. On the other side were rows of black bags waited for those who were gone.

I saw several NYTF officers standing at the edge of the cordon. Understandably, none of them looked happy. This was an attack on their own. They would be extra twitchy to put some rounds in whomever or whatever they thought was responsible.

A few of them gave me silent nods, but none of them looked willing to engage in a conversation. I turned slowly and took in the scene. I was standing in the middle of a war zone. The entire corner building that was the NYTF had been obliterated. It looked like the attack was focused on the second floor—the NYTF offices.

"Ursula mentioned survivors. How many do you think survived *this*?" I asked Monty as we stepped closer. "I mean, most of the building is gone."

"The odds are slim that many did," Monty said, narrowing his eyes as he took in the damage. "There is extensive runic residue in the area. This doesn't read like a Mourn attack."

"How do Mourn attacks read?"

"They don't," Monty said. "The Mourn are siphons—their attacks are detected by the *absence* of runic energy. They leave a void of energy."

"So something *not* Mourn attacked," I said, taking in the extensive damage. "Something strong enough to reduce a stone building to rubble. What do we know that can do this?"

"The list is longer than I would care to consider, but this magic residue...Let's hope I'm wrong. We should see what this message is."

Ursula walked over to where we stood. Next to her was a tall woman I didn't recognize. The way she walked and carried herself told me she was ex-military with extensive training. Her blonde hair was cut short, and her piercing blue eyes told me she had seen things normals would consider impossible.

She wore a black pant suit, dark red blouse, and an

expression that would stop most in their tracks. Like the rest of the NYTF on site, she was upset, and it showed.

The woman held out a hand and I took it. We shook briefly before she exhaled and spoke.

"Jarman, Kathy Jarman, acting director on loan from the Washington State Task Force." She glanced down at Peaches. "Is that a dog?"

"More or less," I said, patting Peaches on the head. "He's a special breed. His name is Peaches."

"Peaches? Really? I've never seen that breed in my life. Is he trained?"

"Define 'trained'."

"Is he going to run through my crime scene contaminating evidence?"

"No, he goes where I go and he'll stay by my side."

"Good. Make sure he stays close," she said with a short nod before looking down at Peaches again. "What breed did you say he was again?"

"Washington Task Force?" I said, changing the subject before she commented on Peaches' glowing eyes. "They went across the country to bring you in?"

"I ported in this morning, Director Ramirez and I go way back," she said, glancing at me, Peaches, and Monty in turn. "We went through training together. He's a good friend and a better director. You must be Strong—Angel has mentioned you and your detective agency a few times."

"I've never heard of any other task force."

"Task Force policy. We don't discuss or divulge the details of other jurisdictions," Jarman said. "Keeps information contained."

"Then why are you here?" I said. "Angel has never mentioned you."

"I'm not surprised," she said. "NYTF likes to think they single-handedly save the world. They don't. We get our fair share of world-ending scenarios out west. We just don't brag about it."

"So you're the Director of the WTF? Really?"

She narrowed her eyes at me.

"I'm a lieutenant and acting director here. Due to the nature of this attack, the Brass felt it was better to bring someone from outside the NYTF."

"Are you saying the NYTF has a leak?"

"I'm saying the itinerary of a director is closely guarded, and this happened while Ramirez was on site. I don't believe in coincidences, and neither does the brass. *That's* why I'm here."

She gave me a look that said *drop it* and I did. If the NYTF had a leak, this wasn't the time or place to discuss why someone would want to set up Ramirez. I made a mental note to bring it up later when I saw Angel.

"Understood," I said, turning to Ursula. "Can you show us this message?"

"This way," Ursula said, leading us deeper into the rubble that had once been the NYTF hub. "None of my people could make out what it said except for the first part. I think you'll agree it was meant for—"

"Shit," I said when Ursula came to a stop. "Is that blood?"

"Yes," Ursula said. "Several bodies' worth."

We stood in front of one of the few remaining walls that were still intact. From the streaks of blood along the floor I could tell several NYTF officers had breathed their last near where I now stood. I noticed the claw marks on the walls and floor.

Someone, or something—I was leaning more to something—had killed them and dragged their bodies to this wall, to use their blood to send us a message. The message covered the wall in a jumbled mess of lines and squiggles.

Like Ursula had said, it was divided into two parts. The first part was mostly lines and curves. The second looked like some kind of hybrid hieroglyphs made of symbols instead of figures.

I couldn't read either.

"Your people could read this?" I said incredulously as I stepped closer to the wall. "I can tell it's two different messages, but there's no way I can tell you what it says."

"I wasn't expecting *you* to," Ursula snapped. "Unless you're proficient in ancient Aramaic. That's the first part"— she pointed to the top half of the blood-soaked wall—"but it's the second half we're having trouble with. Tristan?"

"That's to be expected," Monty said. "It's the cuneiform of proto-Sumerian, a dead language not written for thousands of years; four to five thousand to be precise."

"You can understand this?" I said, surprised. "Let me guess, Aramaic and Sumerian were required languages at the Golden Circle?"

"They were part of the study of ancient languages, yes. Some very powerful castings were written in these languages to prevent their use. Deciphering the second half will take some time. My cuneiform is rusty at best."

"What does it say?" I said, stepping back. "The top part, at least."

Monty stepped closer to examine the wall.

"'The blood', or spirits, of these innocents—it's a little difficult to get a literal translation—belongs on the hands of the bonded immortal, and the golden mage of the circle. The wrath of he who comes will be brought down upon you. Prepare for your end."

The rage inside me rose. Someone had slaughtered this group of people to *send us a message*. My jaw flexed reflexively as I took a deep breath and let it out slowly.

I would make sure they regretted doing this.

"That's what my people made out," Ursula said. "Who did you piss off this time?"

"We haven't pissed off anyone called 'He Who Comes'."

"That you know of," Ursula said. "That probably isn't his formal name. It sounds more like a title."

"Most of the entities that want to stomp us have proper names," I snapped, letting the anger get the best of me. "They don't go for this pretentious BS."

"This wasn't a Mourn attack," Ursula said, turning to Kathy. "There's too much residual runic energy on-site. Whatever did this, is not relevant to DAMNED. Sorry."

"You're pulling your people?" I said, looking at Ursula. "Do you realize we're standing in a crater that used to be an office?"

"I pulled most of my people shortly after the attack," Ursula said, her voice sharp. "The DAMNED is stretched thin as it is." She looked around at what used to be the NYTF hub. "Unless you want to see this devastation on a larger scale—say, most of downtown—my people need to get back to protecting the nexus points."

"I can't believe you're just walking away."

"I can provide you some support personnel," Ursula said, turning to Jarman and ignoring me. "It won't be much, but I can leave some nulls on site. I have to focus on the nexus points."

"Understood," Kathy said with a short nod. "I appreciate any help you can provide. I will get the rest of the NYTF forensics team on this. For now, the official cause is unknown until further notice."

"Would it be possible to get a copy of—" Monty started.

Kathy handed him a sheet of paper. It was an impressively clear picture of the wall.

"Figured you would ask. Anything you find out, you relay to *me* first. Understood?"

"Completely," Monty said. "I will have to reach out to my sources, but I can do so without divulging the details of the case."

"See that you don't," Jarman said. "I don't need to tell you how you will be viewed if word got out that you two had something to do with these deaths, directly or indirectly."

Ursula turned and began heading back to the Widow. I made to follow her when Monty tapped me on the shoulder.

"I suggest you give her some space."

"I will," I said. "I just need to ask her something. Be right back."

I caught up with Ursula, with Peaches padding silently by my side. I looked over my shoulder to see Monty shaking his head.

I was never one to listen to good advice. Why start now?

"What are you doing?" I said as I caught up to her. "They need you here."

"No," she said, turning to face me, "they need you and *Tristan* here."

"People have been killed, good people, and you're just walking away?"

Ursula stepped close and let out a low growl. I realized in that moment that her intimidating presence wasn't a factor of distance. She was scary from a distance and up close.

A little scarier up close.

"I bury good people almost every night," she said, keeping her voice low. "You don't get to tell me what I *need* to do and where I *need* to be. You think this is bad? You better pray the DAMNED never fails or fall, because if we do, this carnage will just be the appetizer on a menu of death and destruction you can't begin to imagine."

"I just thought—"

"Don't," she said, cutting me off. "When you're off tearing my city apart, you don't see me rolling in to interfere with whatever it is you and Tristan are facing. I stay out of your way and deal with the aftermath."

"Yes, but—"

"Are you suicidal?"

"Excuse me?"

"I. can't. believe. you. are. this. dense," she said, each word emphasized by a poke in my chest. "No one who enjoys breathing provokes an angry bear. Stay out of my way and I'll stay out of yours. Now, I have a shift to prep for—this conversation is over."

She turned and left before I could respond. Peaches nudged me in the leg, nearly knocking me down.

<Why did you make the bear lady angry?>

<She's leaving.>

<Because you made her angry.>

<I wasn't trying to. I was trying to get her to stay and help.>

<She can't help. This is not her place. She has to help in her place, and we have to help here.>

<You're right. How are you so wise?>

<I eat plenty of meat. If you ate more, you could be wiser, too.>

<I'll keep that in mind.>

Humbled by Ursula and schooled by my Zen Master hellhound, I rejoined Monty, who was discussing some of the details of the wall with Jarman.

It was then that I made a startling observation.

"Excuse me, Kath," I said. "I noticed you're wearing a red blouse."

"Simon…" Monty said with a sigh. "You'll have to excuse him. He has an acute case of terminal rudeness."

"No, go on," Kath said. "And the name is Jarman, or Director Jarman."

"Right, *Director* Jarman, I noticed you were wearing a red shirt…um blouse. You don't happen to have Scots ancestry, do you? Your name isn't really McJarman, is it?"

"Not to my knowledge, why?"

"Just curious. May I suggest a wardrobe change? Redshirts have low life expectancies where I come from."

"I'll take my chances," Jarman said. "Anything else?"

"I'll make sure to get you any information we uncover as soon as possible," Monty said, grabbing my arm. "Once again, apologies."

"No need," Kath said, as Monty started pulling me away. "Oh, and Strong?"

"Yes?"

"Where I come from, the female redshirts outlived the males. In fact, every female *I* recall with a redshirt worked on the bridge and kicked ass. They were smart enough to avoid away teams."

"Good point, but why live dangerously? Basic black is classic. I mean—"

"Simon," Monty interrupted in a semi sing-song voice, "we have people to see."

I nodded to Jarman and headed back to the Dark Goat. The tone in Monty's voice let me know something was going on. I waited until we were in the Dark Goat.

"What's going on? What people do we need to see?"

"Did you notice the claw marks?"

"I did," I said, starting the engine of the Dark Goat, basking in its deep rumble. "Not Mourndogs or hounds?"

"No," he said. "I fear it's something similar to what you encountered during your ill-fated attempt at hellhound training."

"Hey—hellhound training was your idea, not mine."

"Be that as it may," he said waving my words away. "Do you recall the creatures you encountered? Creatures designed to stop hellhounds?"

"There is no way I could ever forget Shadowhounds. Are you saying they attacked the NYTF? They didn't strike me as self-directed."

"You recall I said the runic signature was familiar?"

"Yes, you were being all cryptic a little while ago, getting your Sherlock on," I said. "Still don't know what you meant. Are you saying it's not Shadowhounds?"

"No. Something worse."

EIGHT

"Where to?"

"We need to confirm what these creatures are, so Haven, please."

"Are you sure? Roxanne wasn't completely on board with releasing you last time."

"It's been some time and you haven't blown anything up. She'll be fine."

"I haven't blown anything up?"

"I just said that. Besides, we're just going to have a chat with Ramirez, if he's conscious."

"And if he's not?"

"I have other methods at my disposal of getting the information I require."

"Do any of these methods require or contain the explosive detonation of property?"

"Of course not. I'm trying to get information, not explode his brain," Monty said. "However, that would be an interesting application. I'll have to see if Professor

Ziller has any treatises on the weaponization of mental probing."

"Can we not explode Angel's brain? What are you trying to find out, anyway?"

"What he saw. It's a simple matter of accessing his visual cortex and sifting through the information of the attack. This can only be done while the subject is alive, so we are fortunate in that regard."

"You worry me sometimes."

"Rubbish," Monty said, waving my words away. "This is a basic cast. We used to use it as apprentices before finals at the Circle. Saved us time on having to read multiple texts."

"Sounds like a Vulcan mind meld to me."

"You have consumed too much television," Monty said. "You realize that's fiction? That there's no such thing as a Vulcan *anything*? Just like your fixation with this fictional non-existent Force."

"It's not a fixation," I countered as I swerved around morning traffic. "I am one with the Force and the Force is with me. Yat told me so."

"Master Yat said this? He uttered those exact words?"

"Well, not exactly. He more or less expressed it with his staff, forcefully."

"Energy is real. The Force, or whatever you want to call it, is fiction."

"Says the mage who can create orbs of energy in his hands, right."

"As I said...energy. Not the fevered fantasies of a film-maker. The Force indeed."

"Maybe Lucas was a mage? Did you ever stop to consider the possibility?"

"No. Never. We have more pressing matters at hand."

I remained silent for a few seconds. I briefly looked in the rear-view mirror as my sprawlificent hound caught my attention with a gentle snore which resembled chainsawing through a forest of redwoods.

"Do I even want to know what's worse than Shadowhounds?"

"Not particularly, no. Do you recall my Reckoning?"

"Are you talking about the day TK kicked your ass? Yes, I remember it. She wiped the floor with—"

"I was there," Monty interrupted. "Thank you. Do you recall who was in attendance?"

"It wasn't that large a group, but all of them were scary powerful. I was mostly focused on not saying or doing something that would get me killed as your shield bearer."

"A monumental feat you managed to pull that off."

"Thanks. LD was a big help."

"Try to recall those who were there to witness the Reckoning," Monty said. "Those who were there for TK. The Triads."

"Well, *you* had Dex, Michiko, and Jimmy the Butcher. Mage, immortal, and shifter, right?"

"Correct—and TK?"

"She had Kristman Dos, the were-tiger, and the scary Morrigan Badb Catha," I said with a shudder. "Have you told Dex about your deal with her?"

"*Our* arrangement, and no, not yet," Monty said. "That's not a conversation I'm looking forward to."

"Do you think he's going to be upset?"

"He's a Montague. He's going to be livid and possibly violent."

"Shit. Can't you explain—?"

"No. On this subject he has always been expressly clear. I went against his counsel. It will not go well."

"He's your uncle, and he loves you. It can't be *that* bad."

"Uncle Dexter is too strong and unstable for the Ten, some of whom you have met," Monty said. "Do they strike you as weak, or as paragons of stability?"

"Not really, no."

"He is currently altering the position of purpose of the Golden Circle, an ancient sect of battle magic...because he wants to, and more importantly, because no one in the sect can stop him. No one."

"Aren't there the elders or some group of grumpy mages that can step in and check him?"

"They've tried," Monty said. "He's stronger than all of them, *collectively*."

"That doesn't sound good," I said. "I mean, he's basically a good person, right? He's not going to try and take over the world...is he?"

"Not to my knowledge, no," Monty said with a slight shake of his head. "Yet, as the Harbinger with Nemain, he fought side-by-side with the Morrigan. They were unstoppable. The only reason he stopped was because pantheons, please note the plural—*pantheons*—became involved, advising him he was on the wrong course."

"He listened to their advice?"

"Of course. It was less advice and closer to 'we will terminate you'. That was the only time he considered slowing down. My uncle is dangerous, powerful, and mostly sane. Frankly, I'm surprised they haven't eliminated him in a pre-emptive, surgical strike."

"Probably more trouble than it's worth," I said. "Are

you sure he expressly forbade you from making any deals with Badb Catha?"

"My uncle is many things, but there is one thing he is very clear about."

"Walking around half naked?"

"No, that's his default."

"Over-sharing his romantic interludes with the Morrigan? Because I could use less of those in my life, really."

"I doubt that will ever change, no. He is very clear about keeping the family clear of divine intervention. It's why he stopped when they threatened him. You think you dislike gods and their games? Uncle Dex abhors dealing with them."

"But...he's with the Morrigan?"

"The Morrigan, not Badb Catha."

"They're the same, aren't they?"

"Yes and no. It's complicated, as is my uncle."

"As is my life," I said with a sigh. "You are in deep shit, then."

"Actually, no. *We* are in deep shit, once he finds out."

"Whoa," I said, nearly swerving into a bus. "What's this *we* business? He's not *my* uncle. He's *your* uncle."

"True, but as *my* shield-warrior, he'll probably blame *you* for my making the arrangement," Monty said with a slight smile. "You really need to take your shield-bearing responsibilities seriously."

"You *cannot* be serious," I said, raising my voice. "How is he going to hold me responsible?"

"He will, O 'Marked of Kali'. Now, focus—who was the mage for TK's Triad?"

I thought back to the memory with another shudder.

"It was that super creepy mage, the one even LD had a

healthy respect for. The dark mage, one of the Soul Renderers. Money or Manny was his name."

"His name is Mahnes. Mahnes the Renderer."

"That's what I said. LD said he was super dangerous and lethal."

"Not was—is. Soul Renderers are mages who have been consumed by dark magic," Monty said. "When you see Roxanne concerned about my use of blood magic, *that* is the root of her concern."

"Grey Sneakers is a dark mage. Does that mean he's dangerous?"

"He is."

"But not Renderer dangerous?"

"Soul Renderers have surrendered to dark magic," Monty said after a pause. "They consume life force to execute their casts. It's one of the darkest forms of magic, and also one of the most dangerous."

"Is Grey that dangerous?"

"Yes, but not because he's a Soul Renderer. He wields an immensely powerful blade that can subjugate his will if he's weak. If that were to happen..."

"You'd have to stop him?"

"I promised him I would. I will keep my word if the need arises."

"Does Roxanne think you're going to turn into another Mahnes if you keep using blood magic?"

"Yes."

"Is she right? Can you turn into one of these Soul Rending mages?"

"Renderers are partially inhuman," Monty corrected. "It takes much more than prolonged use of blood magic to catalyze that transformation, to say nothing of the power involved."

"That doesn't answer my question. Can you turn into Monty the Soul Renderer?"

"I don't possess that kind of power, nor do I possess the inclination to do so," Monty said. "I enjoy being human."

I let out a small sigh of relief I hadn't known I'd been holding in.

"Why are we discussing the creepy Soul Renderer again?"

"Because the energy signature I detected at the NYTF hub was familiar," Monty said. "Signatures are like fingerprints. They can define the cast and the user of the runic energy."

"What are you saying? Tell me you're not saying what I think you're saying."

Monty nodded.

"The signature at the NYTF hub belonged to Mahnes."

NINE

We pulled up in front of Haven.

"Are you shitting me? You can't be serious, because if you are, I want out of this nightmare—now."

"I'm serious," Monty said, getting out of the Dark Goat. "I doubt it was him personally; more likely his minions the Soulless or Unbound, who attacked the hub."

"Is that supposed to make me feel better?"

"Marginally. If it had been Mahnes, we wouldn't be here to visit Ramirez. We'd be burying what was left of him. Let's go."

"Wonderful," I muttered to myself. "This just keeps getting better."

Monty headed inside Haven as Peaches stretched before jumping out of the Dark Goat. The car see-sawed for a few seconds, and I stared at him.

<You're going to need to exit the car gently. Do you know what decorum means?>

<Can I eat it?>

<Can you...No, you can't eat it. It means having manners and

being polite. You need to learn some decorum, especially when getting out of the Dark Goat.>

<Why? The car won't break. You said it can't break, ever.>

I was about to answer when I realized I may have solved Cecil's problem with the Dark Goat. If I just left it with my hellhound, there was a good chance it would be reduced to parts after a few days.

We headed toward Haven's entrance.

<It can't break, but it can't hurt for you to have manners. You know, get out of the car slowly, like a proper hellhound?>

<What is a proper hellhound? I think I am a proper hellhound. How many hellhounds do you know?>

<Two.>

<Two? What other hellhound do you know? Is he proper?>

<I met your dad once, and he was a proper menace. On second thought, let's discuss decorum later. We need to go see Roxanne, so behave. Remember what she said about you and her lobby last time.>

<I gave her lobby some decorum?>

<I don't think that word means what you think it means. If you behave, she may even make you some meat.>

<I always behave. Like a proper hellhound.>

<That's what I'm scared of, boy. Let's go.>

There was a new security team in the lobby. I stepped up to a large desk and heard a familiar voice over the radio.

"He's cleared," the voice said. "Send him up with his pup."

Apparently the security cameras in the lobby had gotten an upgrade. I looked up and waved. It was good to see they were on the ball this time.

The last thing I wanted was a repeat of my last visit to

Haven's lobby and the renovation project which started with my getting hit by twitchy Knocker mages.

I saw Monty sitting in the lounge, which surprised me.

"Why didn't you go up?" I said as he stepped next to me at the elevator. "I'm sure you're a vetted visitor."

"I wanted to make sure the lobby remained the lobby after you left it," Monty said. "The last thing I need is an upset Roxanne because you chose to let your creature redo the lobby...again."

"You only say that because you're probably going to piss her off...again."

The elevator doors whispered open and we entered.

"I've been told that Ramirez is out of ICU, which is good," Monty said. "Hopefully, he'll be conscious."

"What floor do they keep the easily irritated NYTF directors on?" I said, looking at the button panel. "Maybe Roxanne put him on the detention level?"

"Seventh floor," Monty said, pressing the button. "He's still recovering, and that floor is heavily secured. A director of the NYTF is considered a high-value target."

"Seventh floor? High-value, but not *deluxe* value."

"Whatever are you getting on about?"

"Just saying," I said with a shrug. "I doubt Ramirez is going to have his own wing with a squad of sorcerer security guarding his palatial room. Did you know there are some patients in Haven who get the special VIP Deluxe treatment?"

"That squad turned out to be a group of traitorous scum working for your associate, Douglas, if I recall."

"They were, and they got the deaths they deserved," I added. "All except Elias. I liked him. He was tough."

"Indeed," Monty said. "I made sure Haven kept him on

as head of security. He's quite formidable and a pleasant enough person...for a sorcerer."

The doors to the elevator opened on the seventh floor and I found myself face to face with Elias Pirn, aka Paul Bunyan. I didn't think it was possible, but he appeared to have gotten larger.

"Whoa, we get an escort? Since when?"

"Most likely since the last time you were on the premises and you decided to remodel the lobby in your favorite interior design style."

"My favorite style?"

"Nouveau demolition," Monty said. "With an element of annihilation. I hear it's all the rage."

"Oh, early-morning drollery," I said, glaring at him. "I thought you lost that after the schism. So nice to see it's still there."

"My pleasure," Monty said with a brief nod before turning to Elias. "Good morning, Elias."

"Good morning, Mr. Montague," Elias said. "Director DeMarco will join you shortly. She is currently in a meeting with the other facility staff and expresses her regret in not being here to escort you personally."

"Thank you," Monty said. "You're looking well."

"Thank you. This way, please," Elias said. "Director DeMarco informs me you're here to see a patient."

"We are," Monty said. "Director Ramirez of the NYTF. Do you know his condition?"

"He was admitted yesterday and placed with a special security detail. He's stable, but from what I understand, it was touch and go when he arrived. I'll let Director DeMarco fill you in on the details."

We stepped out of the elevator. Elias turned and led us

down the corridor. I had to take the long way around Elias to continue down the corridor.

It was all I could do to resist the gravitational pull. He was wearing a tailor-made, dark-blue suit, paired with a crisp off-white shirt and completed by a dark blue tie. It wasn't one of Monty's Zegnas, but he was pulling off a fairly decent mage impression.

"Nice upgrade. What happened to the combat armor?"

"Director DeMarco felt it sent the wrong message. This is a hospital, after all, not a battlefield."

"Could've fooled me with the number of attacks we've dealt with while we were...Oh, *that's* why you're here."

Elias gave me a short nod without turning around.

"Director DeMarco would prefer the property not suffer any catastrophic...alterations," Elias said. "I've reviewed the surveillance footage. It seems that every time either of you visit, either alone or together, the facility suffers significant destruction."

"Coincidence?"

"Once or twice, maybe. Every time you are on the premises? Causality."

"The last time, I seem to remember some of the destruction was courtesy of your crew."

"That was *not* my crew," Elias said, his voice dangerous as he turned. "Do not, *ever*, associate me with those who tried to destroy this facility. Understood?"

"Understood," I said as we continued walking. "You have a new crew?"

"New crew, new firm, yes."

"Good for you," I said. "What's this new firm? Sorcerer Security?"

"What kind of name is Sorcerer Security?" Elias asked as we walked.

"A poor one," Monty added. "This is why you didn't name the agency."

I waved their words away. It was apparent they wouldn't recognize my creativity if it smacked them in the face with a massive orb of obviousness.

"I have the perfect tagline. Sorcerer Security: 'When it all goes to hell, we'll make sure to get you through'."

"That is absolutely horrible," Elias said. "You should stick to what you're good at—just not while you're in here."

"This new uniform, is it runed? Looks fairly upscale. Not Zegna upscale, mind you, but still, looks like it can handle damage."

"Is he always this...?" Elias began, turning to Monty.

Monty nodded wordlessly.

"Intuitive?" I finished. "Yes, I've been gifted with a keen and sharp mind."

"I was going to say annoying," Elias said. "Yes, it's runed, and we don't have the budget for a Zegna anything."

"Looks like you've been staying in shape," I said. "What are you benching now? Three, four tons?"

"We train the mind and the body," Elias said, glancing over his shoulder. "You're welcome to join us anytime."

"I have a strict policy about pain."

"Really?"

"Avoid it whenever possible, and outsource it when I can't avoid it," I said. "Your training looks painful."

Elias smiled.

"The crucible of pain is good for you," Elias said.

"Burns off the dross and leaves you pure. Only in pain do you discover who you are at your core."

"See? That's why I don't need to train," I said. "I already know who I am."

"Do you?" Elias said, pointing to the door in front of us. "This is where I leave you. Two of my agents will guard the door."

"Two? I thought NYTF Directors were high-value targets? Will two be enough?"

"Elevators don't stop at this floor without security clearance. I think you'll find our security measures more than adequate. Please have my people contact me if you need anything."

"You never did tell me the name of your firm—you know, in case I need extra security?"

"Extra security?" he said, glancing at Peaches. "Why would you need extra security when you're bonded to a hellhound?"

"Occasionally, there are extenuating circumstances that require extra firepower," I said, glancing at Monty. "I'm sure you've encountered a few of those."

"There are some contracts even *I* would refuse," Elias said. "Yours would be at the top of the list, but if you ever find yourself in an *extenuating circumstance* with no one else to call...reach out."

He reached into the inside pocket of his jacket and handed me a blank white card.

"Oh, I see this is some kind of existential sorcerer wisdom at work," I said, examining the card, which was blank on both sides. "What's this supposed to signify, the pure state of mind required? Do your customers need to be a blank slate or something?"

"The name of the firm is Elias Pirn Security," he said. "If you can't read the card, then we aren't the firm for you."

"Next you'll be asking me to snatch a pebble from your hand," I said, still looking at the card. "You can't build your business on gimmicks, you know."

"It's not a gimmick, it's a method of screening clients. Mr. Montague can explain it to you. Now, I have to oversee some other matters—have a good day."

He headed back down the corridor as two well-dressed agents headed our way. The two agents approached and parked themselves on either side of the door. They both looked like smaller versions of Elias and possessed serious energy signatures. He wasn't kidding when he said he trained his crew.

"Let's see if Angel is up," I said, pushing on the door and entering the room.

TEN

Ramirez' room was nowhere near the setup Monty had when he was a priso—patient at Haven. It was a step above a normal hospital room, as befitted his status of NYTF Director, but it didn't even come close to the room Roxanne provided for Monty.

Ramirez slept in the only bed, which dominated the center of the room. Three chairs sat opposite the bed, and a large television hung on the wall above the chairs.

There was a small conference table with more chairs around it on the other side of the large room. I noticed the lack of a library and high-end furniture, along with the ogre-sized hospital bed. On the wall to the right of the bed, I noticed a large window. The glass seemed to be treated, and I managed to see some softly glowing runes etched into it as a safety measure.

Around the bed, were several devices monitoring Ramirez's vitals—at least I assumed that's what they were doing. At regular intervals, a different machine would create some beep or noise or show his pulse and blood pressure.

Ramirez was bandaged up extensively. His face was mostly one large bruise and one of his arms was resting in a soft cast. The skin on the other arm had swelled, and I could tell he had suffered burns along most of its surface.

"He doesn't look too good," I said. "Knowing him, he tried to take on whatever it was that destroyed the hub."

Monty narrowed his eyes and gazed at Ramirez.

"He's suffered significant damage, with several breaks and some internal bleeding," Monty confirmed, glancing at the readings. It was all gibberish to me, but Monty being a Battlemage, would've seen worse.

"How bad?"

"I'm a mage, not a doctor, Simon. At best, I could perform battlefield triage. His condition is beyond my expertise."

"If you saw him in this state on the battlefield..."

"Simon, we are not on a—"

"If you saw him in this state," I continued, "what would you do?"

"I'd try to make him as comfortable as I could, while dulling the pain."

"This...this is not good," I said, looking at Ramirez. "We need to find out who did this to him."

"We will."

"He's family, Monty."

"I know and we *will* do whatever we need to do to make this right," Monty said, his voice hard. "No one touches our family."

I looked around the room, suddenly aware of how alone Ramirez was.

"I told Elias two guards weren't enough. He's in here, all alone."

"Not alone," Monty said, nodding into the corner. "Look closer."

I looked in the direction Monty had indicated. At first, I didn't see anything—but after a few seconds, I saw them. Standing in three of the four corners were three more of Elias' agents.

For the briefest of seconds, I thought they were mannequins when the agent to my right turned to me and nodded. If it was possible, these three read stronger than the two agents standing guard outside.

"Elias takes his security seriously," I said with a satisfied nod. "These guys look serious."

"I would hope so," Monty said, approaching the bed. "Protecting the Director of the NYTF is a grave responsibilty. If something were to happen to him while under Haven's care, the repercussions would be dire."

"Is he awake?" I said, getting close to the bed. Ramirez looked peaceful in his sleep. "He looks like he was chewed up and spat out repeatedly. How did he even survive?"

"We'll have to wait for him to share that with us," Monty said, placing a hand on Ramirez's forehead. "He's in an induced coma. Looks like Roxanne placed him in stasis, most likely to accelerate the healing."

The door opened behind us.

Roxanne stepped in, holding a large mug of tea, judging from the smell, and looking somewhat frazzled. She headed straight for Ramirez before glancing our way. Monty turned toward her.

"Good morning," Monty said, concerned. "How long have you been on shift?"

"A few hours," Roxanne answered after taking a sip from her cup. "Casualties from the NYTF attack have been coming in all night. I've been overseeing logistics and treatment."

Normally, at this point I would give her my rendition of her song by Sting, but seeing Ramirez in this condition robbed me of any desire to sing—unless it was going to be a death song for whoever or whatever did this to Angel.

"You okay?" I said. "Sounds like a long night."

"One of the longest," she said. "I'll be fine and manage some sleep after we have this under some type of control." She glanced down and rubbed my hellhound's head. "Hello, Peaches. You are being especially good today."

<Did you hear that? I'm being especially good.>

<She probably said that because last time you were here you mangled her lobby. Before you ask, I'll ask her for some meat later. Right now she seems tired.>

<I think I deserve extra meat. Don't forget to ask her for extra. I'm a growing hellhound.>

<Let's not push it. You did break her building last time.>

<Frank says one good burn deserves another. Does that mean if I burn the building, I should burn it again?>

Memories of his flame breath flashed in my mind. I shook my head and shuddered slightly.

<It's 'turn' and no burning of any kind inside this building. Keep those flames and any beams in check. No omega beams or flaming barks of any sort. Got it?>

"It's good to see you both," she said, stepping close to the bed and touching Monty's hand. "I apologize for not greeting you when you arrived. I've been tied up in meetings."

"Meetings?" I said, looking out the window. "The morning's just started."

"Not for me," she said. "This attack on the NYTF has raised...concerns among some of the other directors. My morning started shortly after the attack last night."

"Why would this attack be any different?" I said, glancing at Ramirez. "I mean, the NYTF is on the front lines. They know what they're facing. Why are the Directors taking such an interest?"

"The NYTF serves as a vital bridge between our communities," Roxanne said. "They represent an effort to bridge the gap between the supernatural and normal populations of the city."

"If that's the case, why not staff it with a mix of both supernaturals and normals? Wouldn't that be safer for them?"

"We have, they have," Roxanne said with sigh. "Every member of the NYTF is sensitive in some way. To overtly place supernaturals on their staff would be to subvert its purpose."

"Which is investigating and responding to supernatural events in the city," I said. "What aren't you saying? Because from where I'm standing, this isn't out of the ordinary. The NYTF get attacked all the time."

"Yes and no," she said. "Not like this."

"You're going to have to explain this, because I'm not seeing it," I said, frustrated. "Don't get me wrong, I hate that Angel is hurt, and I *will* find whoever or whatever is responsible, and make them regret the day they attacked him—but I'm not seeing the urgency here from Haven Directors. Where were they when Evers blew the place apart?"

"The NYTF is not a supernatural entity like Haven," she said, checking some of the machines and then placing a hand on Ramirez's forehead. A soft red glow flowed from her hand into his skin. "It is not an extension of the Dark Council or any of the sects. It is the normals' response to the things they can't or won't make an effort to understand."

"I get that," I said. "The NYTF is the first and last defense against the things they can't explain. Why does this have the directors' panties in a bunch?"

"This attack was unprovoked."

"Old enemies?" I said. "I'm sure the NYTF has no shortage of those."

"Not at this power level," she said. "The NYTF deals with major threats, yes, but this...this is unprecedented. No hub has ever been destroyed this...completely, with such intent. Then there's the matter of the message that was left."

"The message?" I said with a wince. "You know about that?"

"Yes," she said with a look that indicated I couldn't have seriously been asking that question. "*I* called Ursula once I found out about the message."

"Of course, you would know about that."

"My other capacity, besides Director, requires that I be informed of and contacted in the event of any supernatural crimes that occur in the city."

"I'd say blowing up the NYTF qualifies."

"The Detention area?" Monty said. "Is it secure?"

"We haven't had a breach or an escape," Roxanne said. "Whoever or whatever did this, sent you a message...in blood. Were you able to decipher it?"

"The first half, yes, loosely," Monty said. "It was directed at Simon and me. The second half will take more work. I'll need to brush up on my cuneiform."

"Sumerian?" Roxanne said. "Aren't most of your enemies a little more recent?"

"There may be a few candidates," Monty said. "If we can determine what attacked the Hub, it may make deciphering the second message easier."

"Sumerian cuneiform dates back thousands of years," she said. "Do you know anyone who could read that easily?"

"Yes, my uncle," Monty said. "He has extensive knowledge in languages."

"Of course he does," Roxanne said. "Have you told him yet?"

"About our arrangement with Badb Catha? No."

"I see," she said after a brief pause. "I'll make sure to keep your room prepared in case the conversation goes the way I think it will."

"Any surveillance of the attack?" I said, changing the subject from Dex losing his mind and pummeling us. "Was anything caught by the security cams?"

"To my knowledge, whatever attacked the hub unleashed enough power to destroy the surveillance equipment."

"What could do that? Monty?"

"A massive EMP blast could render the cameras worthless," Monty said. "It would have to be a side effect of the initial attack."

"I don't recall facing anything that releases EMP blasts as a side effect," I said, my voice grim. "You?"

"Let's see if Ramirez can shed any light on who or what

that might have been," Monty said, turning to Roxanne. "Is he strong enough to answer some questions?"

"He should regain consciousness soon."

"How extensive...how bad is it?" I asked, concern thick in my voice. "Will he make it?"

"Every moment he is conscious I have to actively disrupt the signals to his pain receptors," Roxanne said. "If I don't, the pain would make it impossible for him to stay alert. His brain would shut down against the agony."

"How did he survive this attack?"

"Honestly, I don't know how he's still alive or how he survived the attack," she said. "The only thing helping him are the periods of stasis."

"Will he make it?"

"The damage is extensive. It's still too early to tell. Please make this as brief as possible. He needs to remain in stasis for as long as possible."

"Ramirez is too stubborn to die. As long as he's breathing, he's fighting."

"Str...Strong?" Ramirez rasped as he opened his eyes. "Seward...the hub?"

"Hey, Angel, slow it down," I said, putting a hand on his shoulder as he tried to sit up. "You need to rest. You're pretty banged up."

Ramirez rested his head back against the pillow and closed his eyes. Roxanne had one hand extended in his direction and I could see a thin flow of golden energy connecting her hand to Ramirez.

"Can you tell us what happened?" Monty asked. "Who attacked the hub?"

Ramirez opened his eyes and stared at us.

"I don't know," he said, his voice haunted. "It happened

so fast. One moment I was conducting an inspection; the next, one of the walls was blown out."

"Did you see anyone?" I said. "Was anyone strange in the hub with you when it happened?"

"It's the NYTF, Strong," Ramirez snapped. "We have strange on the premises all day, every day."

"You know what I mean. Stranger than usual."

"There was one thing," Ramirez said with a wince as he shifted his body. "The shadows."

"The shadows?" Monty said. "What about the shadows?"

"They came to life," Ramirez said as sweat formed on his brow. "Never seen anything like it, and I have seen some weird shit. The shadows started moving on their own."

"What did you do?" I said. "Can you recall exactly how you responded?"

"Of course. SOP—Standard Operating Procedure. I evacuated personnel from the point of contact, drew my weapon along with several officers, and engaged the enti-ties. We were no match for whatever it was. I led the response and watched my people die."

"Entities?" Monty said after a moment. "You said entities."

"Yes, they looked like shadows, but I can guarantee you that their attacks felt real," Ramirez said. "Nothing we had even slowed them down. It was a massacre."

"Damn," I said. "I'm sorry you had to go through this."

"We know the risks from day one, but I've never faced anything like this," Ramirez said, turning to me. "Who did the brass call in?"

"Kathy Jarman, from Washington," I said. "Any idea

why they would go cross-country to appoint an acting director?"

"No one knew I was going to be at Seward. It was a surprise inspection…guess I'm the one who was surprised."

"Are you *sure* no one knew?" I said. "You didn't have this information on an itinerary somewhere?"

"It was a last-minute change," Ramirez said. "I was in the neighborhood and wanted to pop in, keep them on their toes."

I nodded. It was a normal policy. Surprise inspections worked on the rank and file—especially when the director was someone like Ramirez.

"The brass feels you have…"

"A mole," Ramirez finished. "I know. That's why they brought her in. She's good people. Tough as nails, and competent. Give her all the help you can."

"We will. In the meantime, you need to stay here and recover," I said. "Think you can manage that?"

"Not planning on checking out anytime soon," he said with a grin that turned into a wince as he turned and grabbed my arm with his bandaged hand and became serious. "You find whoever did this. And you make them pay."

"We will."

"On your word," Ramirez said, closing his eyes and resting his head back on his pillow. "Give me your word."

"On my—" I started.

"Not you, Strong," Ramirez said, opening his eyes and staring at Monty. "You. On *your* word. I know Strong. He's like his hound with a bone. He won't let this go until he finds out who it was, even if it kills him, but he can't do it alone. He's going to need help. *Your* help."

Monty nodded.

"On my word as a mage and a Montague, we will find out who attacked you and make them pay."

"Good," Ramirez said with a nod. "Jarman's going to need help too. This isn't Washington. As tough as she thinks she is, they've never faced anything like this. Whoever did this *knows* you two. They've demonstrated they will kill anyone to get your attention. Don't let them take more souls."

"How do you know they know us?" I said. "Do you know about the—?"

"The shadows called you both by name," Ramirez said defiantly, barely above a whisper. "I know no one is going to believe this, but they kept repeating *Montague and Strong*. I don't think anyone else could hear them, but I did."

"Are you sure?" I said. "You heard our names?"

"I'm sure," Ramirez said, his voice firm. "They were whispering your names like a chant as they killed my people. You find whoever did this and end them. You need to keep the NYTF...my city...safe."

"They won't do this again. We'll keep them safe."

"As soon as a the doctor patches me up, I'll be out there with you," Ramirez said with a nod as he closed his eyes again, his breathing becoming ragged. "Right now, I think...I think I need a break."

"He's had enough," Roxanne said and placed a hand on his forehead. A few seconds later, Ramirez's breathing changed, becoming deeper as his expression became more calm. "I hope that helped."

"It did," Monty said. "At the very least, it eliminated some possibilities."

"What he described sounded like the Unbound,"

Roxanne said. "That would mean a—"

"Renderer," Monty finished. "Yes, that is a possibility."

"You can't face a Soul Renderer," she said. "Not without being an Archmage or using…"

"I have no intention of using blood magic," Monty assured her. "We will find whoever it was, and get the necessary assistance if need be."

"If you need help, I'd suggest against employing any goddesses of death," Roxanne said, crossing her arms, her expression dark. "Perhaps your uncle or the Ten can assist?"

"Duly noted," Monty said, glancing at Ramirez. "How is his recovery?"

"He's not out of danger yet,"Roxanne said. "He'll have to remain in stasis until I feel he's recovered sufficiently."

"How long?" I said.

"I still have to monitor his condition," she said. "We're doing everything we can, but I wouldn't expect anything before a few weeks, *with* the stasis treatments. Without them…"

"Got it," I said. "Keep him in stasis as long as you need to. I don't know if he has any next of kin. He's never mentioned…"

"He listed *you* as his next of kin," Roxanne said, her voice low. "Told me there was no one else."

"What?" I said, shocked. "He never shared that with me."

"He was quite adamant about the designation. Apparently he thinks highly of you. Considers you family."

"He is a royal pain in my ass," I said, looking at the sleeping Ramirez, "but he is family."

"I'm sure he feels the same way," Roxanne said, looking

at her watch. "I need to get going. More meetings and more patients. Keep me updated."

"Whatever you need to do, fix him."

"He's in the best facility with the best care," Roxanne said. "Go find out what attacked the hub, and stop it."

ELEVEN

We'd reached the lobby of Haven before Monty spoke.

"We need to go see my uncle," Monty said, looking down at the photo of the wall from the hub. "He will know what this says."

"The Moscow?" I offered. "We can always access his room."

"No," Monty said with a small shake of his head. "We need to meet somewhere safer."

"The Moscow isn't safe?"

"There's nothing there to deter my uncle from blasting us to small particles. No, it's not safe."

"Do you really think he'll be that upset?"

"Yes. He's very adamant about few things in his life. This would be one of the non-negotiable topics."

"What if you explained that you had no other choice?" I said. "We were going up against dragons."

"No choice?" Monty said. "Have you met my uncle? He would consider that response as inadequate—more, he would consider it an insult. I'm a Montague. Not having a choice is a challenge to create one." Monty pinched the bridge of his nose. "I can hear him now: '*When there is no way, you make a way or blow up everything first, then make your way.*'"

"That's the family credo? Explains quite a bit, actually."

"It's *his* life philosophy. Most of the time, it works for him."

"Maybe you should just email. We could avoid seeing him. Actually I'm surprised he hasn't shown up to explode you by now."

"No. He will wait until I initiate the meeting."

"That's good, right? I mean you could always contact him in a few decades and break the bad news. By then he won't be as upset."

"The longer I wait, the worse the outcome will be," Monty said. "Aside from the fact that I didn't consult with him before we made the arrangement, waiting will only anger him further."

"Normally, I'm all for being included, but I can't say I'm comfortable with you saying *we* made the arrangement."

"We did, shield-warrior. No, the Moscow would be contra-indicated, especially if he loses his temper and destroys part of the building. Then, not only will we have to deal with him, but an angry Olga as well. Another location will have to be selected."

"What you mean is we need to meet somewhere he'll be reluctant to kick your ass," I said. "I don't think there are any null zones strong enough to do that, or anyone willing to take that risk."

"I know where, and just the deterrent," Monty said. "It

will, however, have repercussions later on. My uncle doesn't forget or forgive easily."

"Really? Because I doubt Hades is going to arrange a parley between you and Dex," I said, opening the Dark Goat by placing my hand on the hood. An orange wave of energy raced across its surface. I held the suicide door for Peaches, Sir Sprawlington the First, as he entered the backseat—gently, to my surprise. "Good boy."

"I wasn't thinking Hades," Monty said with a raised eyebrow as he looked at my hellhound. "How did you train him to enter the vehicle that way?"

"What way?" I said, starting the engine with a roar. "He is the best hellhound."

"What way?" Monty said. "Like a normal canine, not intent on destroying the rear of the vehicle. Did you promise him meat?"

"We had a conversation about decorum," I said. "Maybe he's finally maturing?"

"I find that highly unlikely," Monty said, glancing behind us at my hellhound. "Is he feeling ill?"

"I'll check."

<Hey, boy? Why did you enter the car so slowly?>

<I'm hungry and haven't eaten in so long.>

<You ate a few hours ago. Your concept of time needs serious work. How can you be hungry?>

<For me, it's always time to eat.>

<Is that why you got in so gently? You're too weak to jump in?>

<Frank says give a little to get it all. If I don't break the car, maybe the angry man can make me all the extra meat I want before I starve.>

<You haven't starved a day in your life. When do you even get a chance to speak to the lizard?>

<Dragon. Frank is a dragon, and he visits me sometimes. Then we talk.>

<The next time he visits, I want you to call me.>

"Well?" Monty said. "Is there something wrong with your creature?"

"Nothing squashing a particular lizard won't cure. He's angling for more meat, as usual."

"Of course he is," Monty said. "You may have to speak to Frank at some point. He seems to be having an inordinate influence on your creature."

"Exactly what I've been saying all this time," I said. "I'm going to speak to Frank...with my fists."

"That method of conversation will go badly for you," Monty said, shaking his head. "I meant speak as in *actual* conversation. Frank seems to have befriended, for reasons unclear to me, your hellhound."

"Befriended? Corrupted is more like it."

"Be that as it may, a conversation—an *actual* conversation, with words, not fists or bullets—is in order."

"I'm going to use words, at first," I said. "Then I'm going to use my fists, or maybe Grim Whisper."

"I'll speak to Grey," Monty said. "That may help."

"Doubt it. Where are we headed?"

"The only place I can have a conversation without my uncle obliterating everything to rubble."

"That doesn't sound like the Randy Rump."

"It's not," Monty admitted. "This is my uncle. We need a place with significantly more stopping power. Besides, I don't think James would appreciate my bringing my uncle to his establishment for another round of 'destroy and rebuild,' even with my runes protecting the space."

"You have a super bunker somewhere that has been ultra-runed that I don't know about?" I said. "Because Dex is off-the-charts strong."

I thought back to when Dex was wielding Nemain, holding open a portal to another plane and fighting me without so much as breaking a sweat.

Not a fond memory.

"There is one place."

The realization dawned on me slowly.

"You cannot be serious," I said. "Why not unleash a nuclear bomb in the middle of a mountain of nuclear bombs? In case you haven't noticed, Dex isn't exactly what I would call stable. Anyone willing to 'date' the Morrigan is high up on my 'batshit insane' list, and you want to take him there?"

"It's the only place I know he won't immediately try to blast me across the continent in a show of familial concern for my well-being."

"Because we'll all be dead first, me included. Have you ever seen him in Harbinger mode? That axe of his is scary."

"I haven't, and to be honest, neither have you," Monty said. "My uncle hasn't been the Harbinger for longer than I've been alive. It was a dark period of his life, one he is reluctant to revisit."

"And you want to take him there?"

"It's the best and only option."

"We are so dead," I said with a groan. "Are you sure we can't create some kind of pocket dimension, or maybe find a plane of peaceful discourse?"

"Don't be dramatic. No such plane exists," Monty said, waving my words away. "We need help with translating the cuneiform, and we need to discuss our arrangement with Badb Catha. Better to rip off the bandage at once."

"Not when ripping it off means you lose your life in the process," I countered. "This is such a bad idea."

"I'll call Ezra and arrange the use of his space," Monty said, pulling out his phone. "I'm sure my uncle will exhibit the utmost tact and diplomacy while on the premises."

"And if he doesn't?" I said. "Because this is *your* uncle we're talking about."

"Then this will be a very short conversation. Either way, it can't be avoided. Head to Ezra's."

I turned on the next street, and heading downtown to Ezra's—and to what felt like certain death.

TWELVE

We pulled up to the rear of a mostly quiet Ezra's and parked in an alley that had been deliberately masked from the general public.

The deli was open at all hours, and now that I thought about it, I had never seen Ezra's closed. What was odd was the foot traffic—or lack thereof.

Usually the morning rush would create a steady stream of patrons entering and exiting the deli. Today, it seemed like everyone was getting their food elsewhere.

The cold grip of fear strangled all of the butterflies in my stomach. Part of me was certain Dex wouldn't go ballistic inside of Ezra's.

No one was *that* crazy...except maybe Dex.

That minuscule amount of uncertainty was enough to make me pause as I turned off the engine of the Dark Goat. If Dex lost it inside Ezra's, what exactly would Ezra do? Did I want to find out?

The answer was no. I really, truly didn't want to find out.

"Are you certain this is the best idea?" I said, stepping out of the Dark Goat. Peaches launched out of the back, caught himself mid-bound, and stepped out the rest of the way. I gave him an approving nod. "Good catch."

"My uncle may have questionable taste regarding the homicidal nature of his partner," Monty said, stepping out of the Dark Goat. "He does, however, know when he is outclassed. This is the equivalent of bringing the bigger gun to the gunfight."

"It's only a gunfight if everyone agrees it's a gunfight," I said. "Bringing a gun doesn't matter if everyone is using RPGs."

"No one is using a gun or any other kind of weaponry," Monty said, pausing at the entrance. "After you."

"I hope you know what you're doing," I said, stepping inside the deli. The runes on the threshold of the entrance flared with violet energy, catching my attention. "That's new."

"What is?" Monty said, walking past me.

"The runes on the doorway," I said, glancing back. "I don't remember them flaring violet when we entered. Orange, yes, but never violet."

"Hmm," Monty said, glancing at the runes on the door frame. "Something to look into at a later date. Right now, let's focus on leaving here in one piece."

"That doesn't exactly fill me with confidence," I said, walking past the tables and the not-so-subtle looks directed our way. I always thought it was a reaction to a hellhound walking into a deli, but this time I noticed some of the looks—actually, most of the looks—were directed at me. "Monty? What's with the looks?"

"Think back, 'Marked of Kali'," Monty said, glancing at

me. "What do you think would suddenly make you popular? It's not your attire or your looks."

"Hey, I'm quite dashing when I want to be."

"It's refreshing to see you have that much confidence, even if you are somewhat deluded," Monty said with a tight smile. "What has changed about you?"

"You mean besides my staggering intellect?"

"If you had given me that answer while we were at Haven I would have requested a thorough examination for you," Monty said with a mild glare. "Now think, as taxing as it may be, on what has *been* changed about you."

It came to me in a flash, and then the cold slap of reality smacked me upside the head, repeatedly.

"Kali?" I said just above a whisper as we headed for the corner where Ezra usually sat. "The mark?"

"Precisely," Monty said with a nod. "Kali *did* warn you."

"Yes, she did," I said, looking around the interior. "Am I imagining things, or does the place seem a little empty to you?"

"It's not your imagination," Monty said, arriving at the table. "I'm sure this is Ezra's doing."

Mori, Ezra's PA, stepped out of the kitchen a few moments later.

"All orders are takeout until further notice," she said, her voice carrying across the floor. "If you're done, please exit the premises. If you're ordering, once your order is fulfilled, exit the premises. Thank you."

I saw a surge in the amount of people who were suddenly finished with their meals. Many of them still stared my way, some giving me unpleasant looks which promised pain as they left the deli.

"Wonderful," I muttered under my breath. "I have a

brand new fan club of 'I want to pound you to death' thanks to this mark."

"Don't think of it as a burden," Monty said as Mori headed to us. "Think of it more as a badge of honor. A lethal badge, but one filled with honor."

"A badge of honor that's going to get me killed?" I said. "Well, that makes it much better, thanks. How didn't I see it? I should be honored most of these people want to kill me. What was I thinking?"

"Precisely," Monty said, looking at the thinning crowd. "Having this many enemies will only make your life more interesting. Imagine: you'll never be bored again."

"Bored? Seriously? My life is anything but boring," I hissed. "Besides, what's wrong with a little boredom? Being bored can be good. No one is trying to kill you when things are boring."

"If I were you, from now on I would operate on the premise that there will always be someone trying to kill you," Monty said. "Operational readiness and all that."

"I'm a detective," I said. "Granted, most of our cases aren't what I would call normal by any stretch of the imagination, but why do I have to walk around ready? Ready for what?"

"Were you not paying attention? Ready for the moment when someone or something does try to extinguish your life."

"Gentlemen," Mori said before crouching down to rub Peaches on his head and chest. To date, she was the only being, besides me, who he allowed to do this. "He's waiting for you downstairs. This way."

Mori was wearing black combat armor, complete with a small arsenal of weapons. I noticed two guns, one in each thigh holster, as well as several short blades resting in sheaths on her legs and forearms, finished off with a longer blade resting in a scabbard on her back.

"Are we heading into battle?" I asked when I noticed the weapons. "You expecting an attack?"

"Let's just say that your new status, and the fact that the Harbinger is paying us a visit, may encourage some unsavory elements to make a move."

"My new status? The Harbinger?" I said, confused. "We're only here to see Dex, not any Harbinger. As for my new status—"

"It's attracting all of the wrong attention," Mori finished. "I'm just taking the necessary precautions."

"They would try to make a move in here? With Ezra on the premises?"

"I didn't say it was a *smart* move," Mori answered as she led us past the kitchen. "However, the Harbinger has no shortage of enemies, and you have a growing hate club. Wouldn't surprise me at all me if those two groups combined somehow to try and take you down."

"Seriously? I'm nowhere near Dex's league."

"True, but the perks of taking you down are considerable. Kali is no slouch when it comes to her favors. Killing the 'Marked of Kali'? Huge reputation builder in the wrong circles."

"Fantastic," I grumbled. "Just how large are these groups?"

"Well, the Harbinger's group is much smaller," she said. "He's managed to cut the number down over the years. They are, however, exponentially more lethal than yours—but hey, you have numbers on your side. Give it time."

"Is that your idea of a pep talk?" I said, shaking my head. "Where did you learn morale building, from mages?"

Mori stopped in front of a large, rune-covered wooden door. I had no doubt that this door was some version of Australian Buloke on steroids. The runes on the surface pulsed with energy as she opened it to reveal a large space beyond.

"I'll be upstairs, just in case it starts to get interesting," Mori said, looking at Monty. "Your uncle hasn't arrived, but he's due any moment. No one refuses an audience with Ezra...for long."

Monty nodded.

"Thank you."

"Don't thank me," Mori said. "Ezra is not pleased. What were you thinking, entering into an unsanctioned agreement with Badb Catha?"

"I was short on options and time," Monty said. "How bad?"

"I'd brace for a good talking to if I were you two," Mori said, heading back upstairs. "Good luck."

"Thank you," Monty said with a wince. "Bloody hell."

"A good talking to?" I said. "How bad can it be?"

"You only say that because you've never experienced it," Monty said, walking forward into the room. "Let's go get this over with."

We entered Ezra's basement.

I had only been here once before, when Ken was looking for Michiko and decided to enlist my help in finding her. I say *enlist*, but it was really more of a demand. There was also the small matter of Monty being on the DCE hit list about his descent into darkness.

This time I was the one with a group after me. It wasn't an organized group like the DCE, but having a group of determined assassins out to make a name for themselves by taking me out didn't exactly brighten my day.

Ezra's basement was a closely-held secret *de facto* neutral zone and meeting area in the city. It was used when supernatural heavy-hitters disagreed on something—usually the wiping out of all enemies—and needed to have a meeting of the minds without blowing everything to dust.

Contrary to what Mori suggested, I didn't think anyone would be suicidal enough to attack Ezra or his deli, unless they really wanted to stop breathing, shifting their status from "attacker" to "deceased" in the span of half a second.

As my eyes adjusted to the dim light, I saw that not much had changed. A large table dominated the center of the space. Seated at the end of the table, radiating an immense amount of power, was Ezra.

He wore a pair of half-moon glasses, and peered at me over the lenses. He was dressed in his regular white shirt with black vest, and black pants. His rune-covered yarmulke gave off a faint violet glow, and he rested his hand over a thick book as usual. It was easy to confuse him with an elderly scholar, and not the personification of Death.

The runes and defensive measures in Ezra's made every other null zone I had occupied look defenseless by comparison. Everywhere I looked, I saw symbols faintly glowing with a spectrum of colors. I remembered Yat's words: *In order to find the flow, you must find a way to work around the obstacles. The runes in this place are a series of obstacles designed to stop the use of energy.*

I tried to find the flow and nearly short-circuited my brain. The runes swirled and swam before my eyes and I nearly collapsed from the information overload. It was a barrage of energy that assaulted my senses, seizing my synapses for a few seconds.

"What are you doing?" Monty said under his breath as he grabbed my arm, keeping me upright. "What did you do?"

"I tried to 'find the flow' around the runes in the space."

"Are you mad?"

"Yat said I should try to find the—"

"Not in this place," Monty snapped. "You'll find the flow right into insanity. Go take a seat and refrain from trying to read the runes in here."

"Don't have to tell me twice," I said and grabbed one of the chairs farthest away from Ezra. If he was in a pissy mood, I didn't want to be in the line of fire.

"Good morning, Ezra," Monty said, living dangerously and picking a chair closer to the old scholar.

Peaches padded under the enormous conference table and made a beeline for the titanium bowl with an engraved P on the side. It was filled with what looked like twenty pounds of pastrami.

<This is why the place is the best place.>

<Try not to eat it all at once. Savor the flavor. Taste it. Don't inhale it.>

<I always taste my meat. Is your mouth broken? Don't you taste your food?>

<Yes. What I mean is, slow down. Take the time to enjoy it.>

<Is this more of the decorum you were talking about?>

<Yes, again. Eating it slowly will allow you to enjoy it more.>

<I don't like this decorum. Can I eat it now? I'm so hungry. I promise to enjoy it even if I eat it fast.>

<Go for it. Make sure to say thank you before you start.>

Peaches rumbled under the table and proceeded to devour the meat in his bowl.

"Good boy," Ezra said with a nod. "Enjoy yourself. As for the morning being good"—he turned to face Monty, then me—"that remains to be seen."

THIRTEEN

"You've both grown in power," Ezra said in a tone that immediately made me feel like I was five years old, had broken my mom's favorite vase, and had tried to hide the fact by gluing it together with Elmer's. "Intelligence, not so much. Explain yourselves."

His look said: *What am I going to do with you two?*

I was transported to all those trips to the principal's office when I broke some rule and got caught. At one point, it was so bad I had my own special chair. Ezra peered down at us over his glasses and waited.

"We were facing dragons," Monty began. "I didn't think—"

"Correct," Ezra interrupted. "You *didn't* think. What about you?" He pointed in my direction. "What's your excuse?"

"What are you talking about?" I said, suddenly upset. "My excuse for what? The fact that we made a deal with the scary goddess, or that the goddess I *do* know and fear marked my forehead with a huge target?"

Ezra shook his head slowly and smiled.

"That mouth of yours...I want to know what was your excuse for letting him"—he glanced over at Monty—"make the deal in the first place. Why didn't you stop him?"

"You wanted me to stop him? Are you serious? How was I supposed to do that? Threaten his supply of Earl Grey?"

"I see," Ezra said. "This is exactly your problem."

"Oh, you *see*?" I said, getting even more upset as I stood. "Well, I'm glad someone sees, because I keep getting fortune-cookie speak and riddles wrapped up in clues that don't make sense."

"Simon," Monty said under his breath. "Remember where you are and to *whom* you're speaking."

"No, Tristan," Ezra said, raising a hand. "Let him speak. Please, go on," he went on, motioning to me.

"I'm tired, I'm confused, I haven't had my coffee and I'm pissed," I continued with the newfound courage of the clueless. "Why is anyone demanding *anything* from me? Did I ask to be cursed? No. Did I ask to start manipulating energy? No. Did I ask for any of this? No. People. Beings. Gods. Should...just...leave...me...alone."

"Simon...?" Monty began and stared at me. "You may want to calm down?"

"NO. I am tired of being told what I should and shouldn't be doing," I said, raising my voice. "Every time a building gets destroyed, somehow it's my fault. What the hell? Since when? When did it become the year of blaming Simon?"

Violet energy surrounded me as I looked down in surprise. The anger and rage I had kept bottled up for so long threatened to explode outward. I looked, glared at

Ezra and he nodded at me with a small smile across his lips.

"Go ahead," Ezra said, waving his hand forward. "You were saying? No one should tell you what to do. Why should you get all the blame? Tell me more. Let it all out."

I screamed incoherently, banging both fists against the very solid table in front of me. Monty leaned back as the violet energy around me grew brighter, even in this null zone.

The energy around me formed a dawnward that expanded, until it abruptly stopped and disappeared. I sat down in my chair, suddenly exhausted.

"I'm...I'm sorry, Ezra," I said quietly. "I didn't mean to..."

"Hush," Ezra said, waving my words away. "You did exactly what you were supposed to do. Feel better?"

"A bit," I admitted. "How did I do that?"

"Nothing a good plate of food can't cure," Ezra said and looked off into the distance. "Your food will be here soon. Now, how did you do what?"

"What do you *mean*? You saw it...the Dawnward. I formed it in here. That's not supposed to happen, not in here."

"Says who?" Ezra said. "Who said this?"

"The buttload of runes on every surface say so," I said. "They're designed to stop that sort of thing from happening. Aren't they?"

"Look at you. An expert on runes all of sudden are you?"

"I just thought..."

"I disabled most of the runes that would have prevented you from expressing yourself," Ezra said. "The other defensive runes are still in place. We do have to let the Harbinger enter, don't we?"

"I don't understand."

"I know," Ezra said gently. "You'd better hurry with the understanding, though. You're running out of time."

"Even with the disabling, he wasn't supposed to be able to do that," Monty said, staring at me. "The runes are designed to—"

"He may have gotten a bit of a nudge," Ezra interrupted. "Stop kvetching so much. Not everything conforms to the rules; you of all people should know that."

Monty raised a finger, opening his mouth to speak, but remained speechless. After a few seconds, he shook his head in surrender.

"It's just that it's impossible," Monty said. "It's not supposed to happen."

"For a mage, no," Ezra corrected. "Simon, however, is not a mage, is he?"

"No, he isn't."

"Good. Now that that's settled, explain yourselves. The Harbinger will be here shortly, and he is none too pleased."

"Well..." Monty began. "The situation was dire. We—"

"No," I said, cutting Monty off. "We don't need to 'explain' anything."

"Simon," Monty hissed. "What are you doing?"

"This isn't the principal's office, and we aren't kids."

"What are you talking about?" Monty said. "Did the Dawnward damage your brain?"

Ezra stared at me.

"We don't need to explain ourselves to anyone, not to Ezra or to Dex," I said. "We did what we needed to do and we saved the city—again, I might add. Why do we need to explain how we did it?"

"This is Ezra," Monty said. "You know, *the* Ezra?"

"I know who he is," I said my voice firm as I stared back at Ezra. "Am I wrong?"

Ezra removed his glasses and pulled out a small chamois. He cleaned the lenses, and for a second, in that small act, I understood. Ezra didn't need to clean his glasses. How could Death, capital D, have poor vision? This was his facade, an illusion he created so our brains could process his immensity, his finality. It didn't require explanation; it just was.

"Technically, no," Ezra said, placing the glasses on his nose. "You're beginning to understand."

I gave Monty a look that said: *See, I was right—so there!*

"What?" Monty said, shocked. "He just can't go around disregarding the requests of beings with enough power to"—he turned to me—"*blink him out of existence with a thought.* There are so many ways that can go wrong. Why are you encouraging him?"

"Also technically correct," Ezra said. "You have to find a balance between the two. Simon, I don't suggest you go around angering gods or beings of immense power. It will end badly...for you. Tristan, loosen the britches a bit."

"I can assure you, my britches fit perfectly," Monty said, and I rolled my eyes so hard I nearly peered into my brain. "Simon's attitude will get us killed."

"Not so much a problem for him," Ezra said, "wouldn't you say? Lighten up a bit and don't take everything so seriously. You"—he pointed at me—"need to take more things seriously. Like how you let this happen. I know you don't know," he added when I opened my mouth to protest, "but you better figure it out, and soon. The Harbinger is here."

A blinding green teleportation circle formed on the other side of the room. When the light dissipated, an angry Dex stood in the center of the circle.

"Nephew." He paused to look at me. "Shield-warrior," Dex said, his voice full of menace. "We need to have some words."

FOURTEEN

"Harbinger," Ezra said. "Sit, please. It's been too long."

"Azrael," Dex said with a nod as he approached the table. "Take no offense as I say it's not been long enough."

Ezra returned the nod.

"None taken," Ezra said, motioning to the chair to his right. "How have you been?"

Dex formed his scary mace-axe, Nemain, and sat in the chair, placing the dangerous weapon silently on the table in front of him. He wore a black suit and I could tell it was similar to Monty's runed, bespoke Zegna outfits.

The suit was complemented by a slate-gray shirt and finished with a deep-green tie. I had never seen Dex dressed up, and somehow this ensemble made him appear even more intimidating than usual.

His hair, which was usually all over the place, was pulled back into a long, braided ponytail. The end of the tail was tied off with a silver clasp in the form of a crow in mid-flight. He glared daggers at Monty and me before turning to Ezra.

My blood, which was doing its best impression of ice water seconds earlier, had completely frozen after that look. It was the look of: *Wait until we get home. You are so going to regret this.*

"I've been enjoying not seeing you, old friend," Dex said after a sigh. "I take it this was my nephew's idea?"

"Do you blame him?" Ezra said with a small smile. "Your reputation, precedes you."

"This, all of this,"—Dex waved a hand—"only means he's a coward," he said, venom in his voice. "He's too scared to face me without you present."

"Monty may be many things," I said, matching his venom, and leaping into the gaping void of self-destruction, "but he is not a coward. Who are you to—"

"Mind your words, *boy*," Dex said with a low growl as energy crackled around him. "I'm the one who wiped his bloody bum before he knew what the loo was. When his father was off fighting monsters, *I* was his father. If he is a man and mage today, it's because of me, and frankly, I'm disappointed." He focused on Monty. "I taught you better than this. I expected more from you. So much more."

I shut up.

This was going to be one of those moments when no matter what was said, it wasn't going to be enough. We were just going to have to take whatever Dex said and deal with it. I could tell from the flexing in Monty's jaw that he wasn't taking Dex's words too well.

Apparently the memo of silence never reached my brain, because the words escaped my lips before I knew what I was saying.

"We did what we felt was right," I said, regretting it

instantly. "What did you want us to do? Surrender to drag-ons? Let them kill us and everyone we knew?"

Dex reached forward and gripped the haft of Nemain, and for a split-second I thought he was going to throw it at me. Even Ezra raised an eyebrow in his direction.

"Harbinger," Ezra said, barely above a whisper. "There will be no violence on the premises."

The fact that Ezra had to say that, scared me shitless. Worse, Ezra said there would be no violence on the premises—that meant anywhere off the premises was fair game for violence.

Right now, Dex looked like he was considering violence with an extra dose of maiming for us.

"Understood, Azrael," Dex said, letting go of Nemain as I breathed out a sigh of relief. "There will be plenty of time for a *deeper* conversation later."

"Good," Ezra said, rubbing his hands. "Are you hungry? We have an excellent selection of meats. Coffee or mead?"

"I'd say this meeting calls for some strong mead," Dex said without taking his eyes off Monty. "Wouldn't you agree, nephew?"

Monty stared back but remained silent.

"Right now I want to know...why? Of all the bloody goddesses, you pick her—and worse, of the three aspects, you pick the bloody Boiling One? You pick the Badb Catha? Have you gone daft? Do you know who and what she is? Even *I* steer bloody clear of her. Why did you do it?"

"She is war, carnage, rage, and violence," Monty said, looking down at the table. "We were facing beings, drag-ons, who only understood the purity of this language. Before you ask, I chose not to get you involved because of your proximity to her. There was no reasonable way to involve you without further complicating an already complicated situation."

"You two have no idea what you've done," Dex said with a sigh, rubbing his face. "You both owe her...*both of you*. Do you know what this means?"

"We both owe her a favor," I said my voice grim. "Both of us."

"I know you think yourselves clever," Dex said. "She is a canny and old goddess. You will not find a way out of this, and if you somehow miraculously do, the way out will be worse than the favor owed. I can't help you, even if I wanted to—and I do, right after I strangle you both for being bloody idiots—but I can't, not in this. You are bound by your words."

"We understand," Monty said. "Thank you, Uncle."

"We do?" I said, confused, and turned to Dex. "What is she going to ask us to do?"

"If you really want to know the answer to that question I suggest you speak to someone who has worked with her," Dex said and gave me a look of pity. "I promise you it will not be a pleasant answer."

"Someone who worked with her?"

"He means TK," Monty said. "She used to work with Badb Catha."

"This conversation is not over," Dex said. "Mo explained why you did it. I wanted to hear it from you. I don't agree, but I understand why you felt it necessary."

"This is bad, isn't it?"

"You have no idea," Dex said, shaking his head. "I'll help you as best I can. It doesn't mean I agree with your decision, but I would be a liar if I said I'd never done something this bone-headedly stupid, or worse."

I shuddered as I thought about what Dex could've done that was worse than owing the goddess of war, carnage, rage, and violence a favor. Then I realized I was the Marked of Kali. On the list of boneheaded and stupid things, I was pretty close to the top.

Monty pulled out the picture Jarman had given him and slid it across the table to Dex.

"What's this?" Dex said, taking the photo. "This looks like...Sumerian? No, proto-Sumerian cuneiform?"

Monty nodded.

"Can you read it?"

One of the waiters came in to the room bringing a large tray covered with food and drinks. He placed it on the table and silently exited. The smell of the pastrami sandwich wafted over and slapped me across the face with the promise of deliciousness.

"I'm starving," I said in my best hellhound imitation. "Ezra?"

Ezra motioned for me to get my food as he sat back. It occurred to me that Monty wanted to meet at Ezra's because if anyone could decipher this, it was Ezra. This was essentially killing two birds with one stone. If somehow Dex couldn't or wouldn't decipher the symbols, he could always ask Ezra.

"Where did you get this?" Dex asked after examining the photo. He slid it over to Ezra, who peered at the photo over his glasses. Dex reached over and grabbed his large mug of mead and sat back. "According to that, you may not have to worry about the Battle Crow, oh, all-powerful 'Marked of Kali'."

"Really?" I said optimistically. "Why?"

"Aye, lad," Dex said, his voice dark. "You won't be alive long enough to worry about her. Your souls will be ripped from your bodies and destroyed long before she gets to you."

"Oh," I said. "That sounds unpleasant."

"Somehow you've managed to get the attention of a Soul Renderer," Dex said. "How did you manage to do that?"

"Mahnes," Monty said. "Perhaps at the Reckoning?"

"Unlikely," Dex said, rubbing his chin. "Did you encounter any during the war, Nephew?"

"Not knowingly," Monty said. "What does the message say?"

"Are you certain you want to know?" Dex said. "It's not good news."

"Yes," Monty said. "At the very least we'll have the knowledge."

"What about you, boy?" Dex said looking at me. "Do you want to know?"

I gave it a moment of thought. Knowing was always better than not knowing. The blow that hurt the most was the one you didn't see coming. Plus, whoever had left this message had hurt Ramirez and killed innocents at the NYTF hub. I wanted to know who it was I needed to dust.

"Yes," I said. "Tell me how we this Mahnes."

Dex shook his head.

"I don't think it's going to be that easy," he said. "I can tell you what the message says, but it's not like it's signed by anyone."

"But you're certain it's a Soul Renderer?"

"I've been around enough of them to know how they speak," Dex said. "Also, judging from the amount of blood used in this message, I would say bodies were drained to create it, yes?"

I nodded.

"They attacked the NYTF, killed several officers and drained them to leave us this message," I said. "This was after—"

"They tore the place apart," Dex finished. "It looked like a bomb went off in the place?"

"Yes. The offices were obliterated. Looks like it was hit with tank fire."

"Soul Renderer, or more likely, his Unbound," Dex said. "Subtle they are not. Nasty pieces of work, though."

"How do we stop them?"

"The Unbound?"

"Yes, how do we kill them?"

"You don't," Dex said. "They're unbound. They have no souls. They feel no pain. Nothing short of complete disintegration stops them. This is a being in thrall to a powerful dark mage."

"Then we stop the dark mage."

"Do you remember when he was in the middle of his schism?" Dex said, glancing at Monty. "He was, and is, fairly powerful now."

"Yes," I agreed. "And scary, too."

"You are facing a person who can siphon the souls of humans and use their life force to power his energy," Dex explained. "Not only that, but this isn't a schism. This is someone who has surrendered to, embraced, and relishes the darkness. This is evil."

"Even evil can be stopped," I said. "Are you saying it can't be?"

"I'm saying that this evil may be beyond you both," Dex said. "There's one more thing. Have you angered any of the old ones?"

"The old who? I know plenty of senior citizens. Most of them are grumpy."

"Simon has," Monty said. "Are you saying this may be a result of that?"

Dex nodded and pointed to the photo.

"Read them the message," he said, glancing at Ezra. "It may help them. At the very least they'll know."

Ezra looked down at the photo and cleared his throat.

"You thought me gone, but I am ever present. I am infinite. I am entropy. I am everlasting. My agent will bring you to me and then, when you have lost all hope, I will rip your souls from your bodies and devour them. In that moment, you will know me. In that moment, you will know utter despair and entropy."

My heart nearly stopped. I knew those words.

"I remember those words," I said. "Monty?"

"Which words?" Dex said. "You know who this is?"

"No," I said. "But I remember facing someone who said those words to me a while back: *I am infinite. I am entropy. I am everlasting.*"

"Are you certain?" Monty said concern in his voice. "Who was it?"

"Karma told me he wouldn't be back for at least a century or more," I said. "It hasn't been a century. I guess he's moving up the timetable."

"Karma?" Dex said confused. "Karma said those words? Since when do you speak to Karma? When did he say those words?"

"She. Karma is a she, and it wasn't her."

"Who, then?" Dex said. "Who did you two piss off enough that he wants to rip out your souls and devour them?"

"Chaos."

FIFTEEN

"Chaos," Dex said, sitting back. "*The* Chaos?"

"He was in corporeal form when I sent him back"—I glanced at Monty—"with Monty's help," I said. "Those were the last words he said to me. 'I am infinite. I am entropy. I am everlasting'."

"Is it possible he has a new agent?" Dex asked, looking at Ezra. "Another vessel that's now a Soul Renderer?"

"A new agent?" I said. "I thought Chaos was a concept, not a sentient being."

"Yes and no," Ezra said. "Order and Chaos are forces of reality. Every so often they personify to subvert the will of the other. When that occurs, balance must be restored, or it will mean The End."

"The end? The end of what?"

"Everything," Ezra said. "There must always be balance...always."

"When I faced him, I faced a bunch of sorcerers," I said. "Are you saying he's in *one* person now? Because that would mean..."

"He's even stronger now," Ezra finished. "To occupy one vessel means this new agent is vastly powerful, and entirely given over to the concept of entropy."

"Wait, why me?" I said. "I mean, I get that I pissed him off in the past, but why come after me now?"

"If you interfered his intention in the past, you were acting as an Agent of Order," Ezra said. "That alone would be a reason, but it can go beyond that. It is possible that Chaos is preparing to enter his Endgame and is being pre-emptive, by removing *you*."

"Aye, and he's removing any potential threats or obstacles to his plan," Dex said. "You two certainly qualify."

"Are you saying Mahnes is being controlled by Chaos?" I said. "Because that sounds like the worst possible scenario ever, of all time."

"No, better than that," Ezra said. "If Mahnes is the new Agent of Chaos, then Chaos is controlling Mahnes, who commands an army of Unbound, focused on destroying you two."

"Thank you so much for clearing that up," I said with a stare as a small, but ever-growing well of panic was starting to form in the pit of my stomach. "How is that better? That's not better, that's worse...much, much worse."

"It all depends on your perspective," Ezra said. "You can choose to see it as an ancient entity bent on your destruction coming to exact vengeance on your past actions, or you can see it as...well...actually, that is the only way to see it. You two are in a pickle."

"Chaos wants to rip out and devour our souls and we're in a pickle?" I said, turning to Monty. "How do we fight him? If we can't kill him, we have to be able to stop him. Another Negation rune? It worked last time."

"It won't work this time," Monty said. "We will need to use something that can work against a Soul Renderer."

"I'm all out of Soul Renderer elimination rounds. I'm open to ideas, though," I said. "What exactly works against a soul-sucking dark mage?"

"We need an etheric tether," Monty said. "Think of it as soul protection. Highly volatile, unstable soul protection."

"That's some nasty business, nephew," Dex said. "If you make one mistake, your souls are lost."

"If we fail to act they are lost, regardless. Do you know where she is?"

"Etheric tether? Where who is? Who are we looking for now?"

"Tessa and the Moving Market," Monty said. "She would have a tether."

"Tessa? The Tessa who tried to blow us up—that Tessa?"

"Yes, that Tessa."

"She and I had...words," Dex said with a scowl. "She'll cause you no direct harm."

"That doesn't sound like we can trust her," I said. "No direct harm leaves plenty of room for indirect harm. I don't trust her, or her Doorman."

"Aye, and you shouldn't," Dex said. "She's dangerous and powerful, but she understands the consequences should she move against you. She'll cooperate with your request. I had Mo pay her a visit."

"You sicced the Morrigan on her?" I said with a smile. "You...are an evil man."

Dex smiled for the first time since he entered Ezra's.

"That I am," he said. "Do not antagonize or give her a

reason to attack, and you should be fine. Besides, Mo rarely gets to have fun these days."

I shuddered to think what the Morrigan considered "fun".

"What about Roque?" I said. "Were you able to help him?"

Dex's face darkened.

"I took care of him."

"You what? Did you...?"

"What? No," Dex said, offended. "What do you take me for?"

"Seriously? The last time we met, you were trying to slice and dice me with that thing in front of you"—I pointed to Nemain—"and today you showed up here dressed for a funeral. I assumed it was ours. What did you expect me to think?"

"I didn't kill him, if that's what you're insinuating, boy. He was in a bad way. I merely helped him deal with the effects of the runic trap."

"What did you do?"

"He's safe for now. His last battle with that Doorman of hers nearly killed him. I managed to relocate him somewhere where dragons aren't used as guard dogs."

"And Tessa? Did you pound her into paste? She tried to blow us up."

"We had a *conversation*," Dex said. "I informed her it would be in her best interests not to harm either of you should you choose to revisit the Market."

"That whole place needs to be shut down," I said, anger lacing my voice. "Are you saying she's still going to be running it?"

Dex nodded.

"Aye, some evils are necessary," he said. "Tessa and the Moving Market do more good than harm."

Every community has a dark side—the face that's kept hidden from the light, and from outsiders. It's revealed in the shadows, when you're out of options or looking to erase any trace.

It's the corner of dark alleys, the whispers of promised vengeance, the impact of a life-ending round between your eyes, or a soul-stealing rune turning your body cold and lifeless before it hits the ground.

The magical community was no exception; its dark side was only more dangerous because of the forces involved. The Moving Market dealt in lethality and the lost—and those wishing to remain that way. If you wanted to disappear, you slid into the Market.

If you were taken there—the end result was the same.

You were gone.

Most of the items sold in the Market qualified as contraband: something to disintegrate a target on sight, a rune to control a person's mind, or information you needed to destroy a rival. You could find it all in the Moving Market—for a price.

"Not seeing it," I said. "Did I mention she tried to blow us up? Plus, she sent the janitor after us. That was fun...not."

"The Janus," Monty corrected. "Not the janitor."

"You deal with her the way you deal with a venomous snake," Dex said, finishing the rest of his mead. "You keep your eyes on it without being foolish and—"

"Chop off its head if it gets too close?" I said. "I'm all for the head-removal option."

"No, you don't destroy a snake for being a snake," he

said. "You respect the danger it presents, use the venom for good when you can, and never turn your back on it."

"Or...you can just burn the snake out of existence. Problem solved, no snake, no venom, no danger."

"You've been spending too much time with my nephew," Dex said, glancing at Monty. "If I were to destroy her or the Market, several sects would be after my head. I have enough worries with just the Golden Circle. No need to add more sects to my causes of headaches."

"Could you? I mean, destroy the Moving Market?"

"I'd rather not have to find out, boy," Dex said, his voice dark. "Make sure you conduct your transaction and exit the Market as soon as possible. The longer you dwell in there..."

"The greater the chance of an attack from Tessa," Monty finished. "We will expedite this as quickly as possible."

"You'll find the Market in the usual places. See that you don't overstay your welcome," Dex said, getting to his feet. "In the Moving Market, Tessa's abilities are...challenging. A duel in her home would be ill-advised."

"We have no intention of dueling her in the Market, or anywhere else for that matter," Monty said, standing as well as he gave me a glance. I got to my feet. "Thank you for coming, Uncle."

Dex gave us a sly grin and looked around as I stood up.

"This was the smart play, Nephew," Dex said, glancing at Ezra, who remained seated. "We still have much to discuss, and I'll see what I can do with the Morrigan, but I make no promises. You sow, you reap."

"Understood," Monty said with a slight bow, which Dex returned. "Will you be going back to the Sanctuary?"

"Ach, indeed. I'll be bringing those stuffed shirts into this century whether they like it or not," Dex said with a mischievous grin. "We'll be preparing battle mages soon enough. Just need to do a bit of restructuring with the staff"—he gave me a pointed look—"after the rebuilding, that is. Apparently *someone* released a runic nova in the middle of the Sanctuary, obliterating it to rubble."

"A runic nova?" Monty said nonchalantly, adjusting the sleeve of his jacket. "You don't say?"

"I *do* say," Dex said, glaring at us. "Not a typical cast, mind you. The rebuilding will be extensive."

"That sounds extreme," I said. "If I hear anything, I'll be sure to let you know."

"*Sure* you will," Dex said. "After the rebuilding, the School of Battle Magic will begin in earnest. The Elders will kick and scream, but they will agree in the end."

"Somehow that agreement sounds painful."

"It will be...for them, if they refuse to accept that isolation is not the answer," Dex said, gesturing and forming a large green circle several feet away from the table. Dex looked around. "Where's the hound?"

"Food coma," I said, indicating under the table. "Ezra insists on keeping him stuffed with dangerous amounts of meat."

"You disagree?" Dex said, peering under the table with a nod. "With Ezra?"

"I try not to fight pointless battles," I said. "He wants him to weigh three hundred pounds and barely fit in the Dark Goat or walk through any normal doorways. Not my call."

"Smart man," Dex said, stepping into the circle. "Your hound is still growing. He needs all the meat he can get."

"That seems to be the plan," I said. "Should I buy a butcher shop when he stops growing?"

"Hopefully his appetite will calm down by then."

"Hopefully? That fills me with so much confidence," I said, turning to Monty. "Maybe Jimmy can do double orders?"

Dex smiled, then grew serious as he looked at Ezra.

"Azrael," Dex said with a slight nod. "May our next meeting be as uneventful."

"Harbinger," Ezra said. "May your weapon gather dust."

"Thank you," Dex said. "May it gather dust, indeed."

With a flash, Dex was gone, and I let out a long sigh of relief as I sat down again. The teleportation circle slowly faded out and vanished.

"Can we not do that again...ever?" I said. "For a second, I thought he was going to use his psycho axe-mace."

"He was," Monty said, taking the seat opposite me. "He was here as the Harbinger, not my uncle."

"Correct me if I'm wrong, but isn't that the same person?" I said. "Your uncle, Dex, is the Harbinger. The Harbinger is your uncle?"

"No," Ezra said. "The Harbinger has a second part to his name."

"Harbinger Montague?"

"You are an incredible pain in the *tokhes*, Strong," Ezra said, shaking his head and getting to his feet. "If you used that thing you called a brain, your life would be so much easier. Finish your food and see yourselves out. I have to make sure the shop reopens. Some of the guests will be anxious to make your acquaintance. I suggest you use the alternate exit. Remember what I said—*both of you*."

He shuffled out of the room, the runes along the threshold of the door glowing brightly violet as he passed them.

"How could Dex attack us in here? With Ezra sitting there?"

"More importantly, how was my uncle able to teleport in here?" Monty said. "The defenses should have prevented that."

"I'm guessing Dex has special access or something?"

"The second half of Dex's title is well known and actually explains his affinity for the Morrigan," Monty said, rubbing his chin. "I can't believe I didn't see the connection before."

"I'm happy you see the connection. Care to enlighten those of us still in the dark?"

"For a very long time... I'm not certain of the exact length of time as this was before I was born, but I heard the stories—my uncle was known as the Harbinger of Destruction."

"Kind of makes sense, actually."

"He has one older title, it's one he never uses: the Harbinger of Death."

"The Harbinger of...Oh," I said as the realization became apparent. "That means he could've—"

"He could have attacked us if he so chose," Monty said. "Only Ezra and his affection for us kept him in check."

"What happens when we see him again?" I said, concerned. "Ezra won't be there."

"Let's hope he still feels enough affection to leave us intact."

"I think you've really missed your calling as a demotivational speaker," I said. "I always feel the situation is a little darker after your insights."

"Mages are realists," Monty said, heading for a back wall. "We need to go see Tessa. Let's go."

"The exit is that way," I said, thumbing over my shoulder to the door Ezra used. "Where are *you* going?"

"Alternate exit, remember?" Monty said, stepping close to the back wall. "Do you want to walk through the seating area again, Mr. Popular Marked of Kali?"

I remembered the stares from the patrons eyeballing the new "Marked of Kali" and making mental threats as we walked in.

"Hard pass on walking the gauntlet of menacing stares again," I said, nudging my snoring hellhound. "The alternate exit sounds like a great plan. Let me get Hurricane Snores up. Give me a sec."

I gently shoved my hellhound and watched him shake himself awake as he focused on me.

<Is it time to eat again?>

<No, it's time to leave. Is that all you think about? Food?>

<No. I think about the Guardian, too, and my naps. My naps are good.>

<What about your bondmate? No thoughts for the bondmate who feeds you?>

<I don't have to think about you. Wherever you go, I go.>

Wonderful—my hellhound was a teenage boy in the grips of a hormone overdose.

<Life is not just eat, sleep, and girls...well, Guardians, you know. There are other things that are more important.>

<Frank says life is simple. The important things are simple. Protect those you care about. Rest when you can, and eat as much as possible.>

For once, I actually agreed with the lizard. Except for the eating part, his advice made actual sense.

<I'm sure you're focused on the eating part.>

<Of course. Meat is life.>

"If you're done conversing," Monty said, "let's go acquire a tether."

SIXTEEN

The alternate exit led to the masked alley behind Ezra's.

"How did you even know about that exit?" I asked as I examined the alley for threats. "Is that a recent thing?"

"Every null zone has multiple exits," Monty said. "It's a safety precaution."

"Even Ezra's?"

"Especially Ezra's," Monty said, placing his hand on the wall and sealing the exit with a soft orange glow. "Considering how most of the patrons reacted to your presence, I'd say it's a necessity."

"I wasn't exactly enjoying the stink eyes either," I said. "I just didn't expect it to have security exits. I mean, Ezra is there. No one is insane enough to cross him or launch an attack in his place."

"Your trust in the better nature of beings is refreshing...and naïve," Monty said. "'Hell is empty and all the devils are here'."

"Did you just Bard me?"

"I felt it was apt," he said as we approached the Dark Goat. "Most of the patrons—not all, but most—dine there because it allows them a moment's respite from the violence of their lives. They are not good nor friendly. They certainly do not have your best interests at heart."

"Especially now, with this wonderful mark Kali gifted me," I grumbled. "Because my life wasn't complicated enough. Now I get to fight off eager idiots trying to make a name for themselves."

"I doubt many would dare approach or confront you," Monty said. "At least, not yet. Although, I am concerned about how powerful your mark may be. Kali is not known for her subtlety."

"What do you mean?" I said. "Is it visible? Can you see it?"

"Not exactly," Monty said, narrowing his eyes as he stared at me. "I don't understand why not. It could be that I'm not the intended recipient and she has somehow managed to mask it from me."

"If you're not the intended recipient, who is?" I said, unlocking the Dark Goat. "On second thought, I'm pretty sure whoever is the intended recipient is going to be unpleasant."

The hammer-on-anvil clang of the lock reverberated in the alley. An orange wave of energy raced across the surface of the Dark Goat as the doors unlocked.

"That goes without saying," Monty said. "Kali is big on her representatives proving their worth. If I recall, you angered her considerably. She isn't going to make this easy."

"*We* thwarted her plan, but *I* get cursed," I said. "How is that remotely fair?"

"You expect Kali to be fair?" Monty asked as he opened the door on his side of the Dark Goat. "What reality do you live in?"

We almost managed to leave the alley without encountering anyone trying to make a name for themselves by proving how badass they were by taking down the Marked of Kali.

Almost.

Monty had settled into the passenger side and my hellhound had found the ultimate sprawl as he stretched out occupying all of the space in the back seat.

I had settled into the driver's side of the Dark Goat, when I heard Peaches growl.

Something stepped behind the Dark GOAT, blocking out the entire rearview. A second later, I heard a voice behind us. It was a deep, low, raspy sound that scraped against the back of my skull and made the hairs on the nape of my neck stand on end.

"YOU are the Marked of Kali?" it rumbled. "Is this a *joke*?"

I stepped out and turned slowly, unprepared for the slap of ugliness as I looked up into the face of an immense and angry-looking ogre at one end of the alleyway, blocking our exit.

"Whoa," I said, catching my breath. "That's a face not even your mother could love. Someone woke up with an extra dose of gruesome today."

As ogres went, he was the standard issue. Huge, with muscles that hit the gym regularly and had muscles of their own. Scary, with a horrific misshapen face that erased the concept of a good night's sleep for at least a decade.

What made this ogre stand out was the subtle orange

glow around his body. That and the fact that he was grabbing the Dark Goat without suffering any side effects.

"Monty," I said without taking my eyes off the mountain of nastiness blocking our way. "Since when do ogres glow?"

"Ogres don't...glow," Monty said, getting out of the Dark Goat. "I stand corrected."

"The glowgre is blocking our way out. I could just run it over and call it a day."

"Ogres are quite resilient," Monty said. "All that would do is anger it."

"Then we'd have an angry glowgre chasing us through the streets. Not a good idea."

"Too much collateral damage. Perhaps it's lost?"

Peaches padded over to my side and let out a low rumble that vibrated in my stomach.

<Don't get too close, boy.>

<Can't I bite the orange monster?>

<Only if it attacks. I think right now it wants to talk.>

<If it tries to hurt you, I will bite it.>

"I doubt it's lost," I said, still focused on the ogre. "Besides, lost on the way to where? This isn't exactly an ogre hotspot. Are you saying it was headed to Ezra's for breakfast and took a wrong turn into the masked alley where we happened to be standing? Seems thin."

"Agreed," Monty said. "There's a good chance someone who saw you inside earlier notified it. Find out what it wants."

"It's an ogre," I said. "Glowing or not, I'm pretty sure I know what it wants. The usual; death, destruction, mayhem, and maiming. They all tend to lean in that direction."

"Always pays to be certain," Monty said, taking a step forward and narrowing his eyes at the creature, before moving back to stand by my side. "It really *is* glowing. Intriguing."

"Thanks for the confirmation, but I can see the glow from here."

"Ogres are creatures of magic, but to my knowledge they haven't been known to manipulate it," Monty said. "This is quite unprecedented."

"Maybe this one is an overachiever," I said under my breath. "Would be my luck, I run into the one and only ogremage."

"That would be unlikely," Monty said, clearing his throat and placing a hand on my shoulder. "May I? I'm curious."

"Be my guest," I said, stepping back. "All yours. Maybe you could use that famous tact of yours and convince it to go back under whatever bridge it crawled out of."

"That would be mostly trolls, not ogres," Monty corrected. "Ogres have a tendency to dwell in old forests. Which makes its presence here peculiar."

"Right, like *any* of what happens in our lives is normal," I countered. "Tell Shrek to go home and we can avoid the whole 'trying to kill each other' portion of the morning."

Monty took another few steps forward, smoothed out one of his sleeves, and let energy flow into his hands. Arcs of deep violet raced around his body. It was a not-so-subtle display of the impressive amount of power he now wielded ever since the schism.

I couldn't tell if the ogre noticed the power Monty was flexing. Its facial expression was stuck somewhere between blood-curdling and disinterested. I did notice that it slightly shifted its focus from me to Monty as he got closer.

"You are not the Marked of Kali," the ogre said in a rumble that mimicked gravel being crushed by a large hammer. "You seek death?"

"I do not," Monty said, stopping his approach some distance from the large mass of ogre monstrosity. "Do you?"

The ogre stared down at Monty and let out a sound that was a cross between a major truck collision and an earthquake. I guessed that's what passed as laughter among ogrekind.

"I will make sure to kill you and the pup second," the ogre answered. "After I drink the Marked of Kali's blood, you will be my dessert."

"How did you find him?" Monty asked, standing his ground and ignoring the threat of being put on the ogre breakfast menu. "How did you find the Marked of Kali?"

The ogre tapped its forehead and smiled, revealing a set of teeth that would make most dentists gouge their eyes out. Those who didn't would instantly lose their minds and start running in the opposite direction.

"The Marked of Kali cannot hide," the ogre said. "The mark calls to me."

"I see," Monty said, glancing back in my direction. "We are quite pressed for time. Would it be possible to postpone this assassination to a more convenient time?"

The ogre stared down at Monty and roared. The deafening sound raced down the alleyway, echoing off the walls.

"Marked of Kali, today you die," he said, followed by a growl. "Today, I feast on your flesh."

"How did it go?" I said, as Monty stepped back next to me. "He seems hungry."

"Wants to feed on you, drink your blood, finish off the meal with me and your creature," Monty said, still staring at the ogre. "Typical ogre behavior. Shed no light on how he found you except to say the mark calls to him. That does not bode well."

I turned to stare at Monty for a few seconds.

"You think?" I said, drawing Grim Whisper. "Sounds like Kali put a monster-homing beacon on me. What happened to, 'I doubt many would approach you'?"

"It's one ogre," Monty said, pointing at the monster. "One is not many. Technically, I'm correct."

"Technically, my ass," I said. "It's one *glowing* ogre. We need to lure it closer to us. If it gets out in the street..."

"That would be unwise," Monty said. "The damage would be catastrophic. I'll leave the luring to you."

"Nice of you, thanks," I said, walking toward the ogre. "You better be ready to unleash some ogre-stopping orbs or something."

"Or something," he said waving me forward. "Go on, lure away."

I stepped as close as I could without placing myself within arm's reach of the ogre. They were large creatures, but moved deceptively fast. At my current distance, I had about two to three seconds before it could reach and pound me into paste. Peaches rumbled next to me.

"You've come to lay your life at my feet. Good," the ogre said, baring its horrendous smile. "I will make your death swift, Marked of Kali."

"About that," I said, making sure it could see Grim Whisper. "I have this condition—"

The ogre didn't wait for me to finish—he charged.

SEVENTEEN

Fighting an ogre in an open space is a dangerous thing.

They have plenty of room to maneuver, can close distances before you can react, and have blazing-fast reflexes. It's a bad scenario all around. The only thing worse than fighting an ogre in an open space is fighting one in a confined space.

They still have all of the above advantages, but now you're in a confined space, which means you can't use the ultimate strategy against it: the subtle art of running away.

I fired Grim Whisper as Peaches blinked out next to me. I was currently carrying entropy rounds. Ever since I realized everything I met was trying to shred me, I decided it was only fair to return the favor before they got the chance.

I managed five rounds center mass, which the ogre shrugged off as if I had been using paintballs. Peaches blinked back in and clamped down on one of the ogre's legs. It screamed and slapped my hellhound away, launching him back down the alley. Peaches blinked out mid-flight and reappeared next to me. He shook his body with a low growl and entered "maim and shred" mode. I noticed his eyes were glowing.

The ogre swung a massive fist and nearly removed my head. I ducked and rolled back firing again, with no effect. The ogre's fist smashed into the wall, leaving a nice fist-sized crater before focusing on me again.

"You cannot escape, Marked One," it said. "I will crush your bones and squeeze the life from you."

"I get the feeling you weren't hugged enough as an ogrelet...ogreling...whatever it is you call little ogres," I said, firing again and switching magazines. "How did you learn to create a shield? You're an ogre. Why would you need a shield?"

"This is my right as your successor," the ogre said. "This is the Mantle of Discord, granted to all who would destroy the Marked One."

"Why don't I like the sound of that?" I said. "Monty? Mantle of Discord? Ring any bells?"

"Bloody hell," Monty said. "I knew that shield seemed familiar. Try not to let it hit you. I'm working on something."

"Entropy rounds are only tickling it," I said, firing again. "I hope you have something that can actually do some damage."

"Let your creature distract it with his baleful glare," Monty said, gesturing. "I should be able to get that shield down and maybe stop it."

"Maybe Peaches can use his Hellfire?" I said, moving back as the ogre closed on us. "He could barbecue it."

"We're in a confined space, and you want your creature

to unleash eldritch flames that burn hotter than any normal flame?"

"Good point. I'm not looking for an insta-tan."

"Baleful glare please, and hold the hellfire," Monty said, gesturing. "Now would be good."

I glanced down at my ferocious hellhound ready to attack.

<Do it, boy! Hit it with your omega beams!>

Peaches barked, shaking loose some of the bricks in the wall and unleashed twin beams of red destruction at the ogre. The orange glow around its body flared as the beams impacted, slowing down its approach.

The ogre growled in anger and pain, but it kept coming.

"I'm going to kill your hound first, and make you watch," the ogre said, taking methodical steps in our direction. "Then I'm going to rip your head off."

"Omega beams aren't doing much," I yelled over my shoulder. "Should I—"

"No!" Monty said quickly. "Do not use anything but your gun."

"I may as well be firing cotton balls at that thing. That sounds like a bad idea."

"Trust me," Monty said. "Tell your hound to stop."

"Stop? That means the ogre will..."

"Yes, I know—tell him to stop."

<Stop beaming the monster. Monty wants to blast him, I think.>
<If I stop, the big monster will try to hurt you.>
<Monty is going to stop it before it comes to that. I hope.>

Peaches stopped his laser beams and the ogre staggered forward as the resistance to his approach vanished.

Monty ran forward past me and unleashed two small violet-red orbs before sliding to a stop and reversing course. The two orbs punched through the shield and into the ogre's chest with a low *thump-thump*. The ogre looked down at his chest and then back at us, roaring again.

"Your weak magic will not save you!"

"Get in the car, now!" Monty yelled as he ran toward me. "Move, Simon, *move!*"

I turned and ran for the Dark Goat. For a few moments, Peaches was behind me, the next, he was inside the Dark Goat sprawled so low in the backseat I couldn't see him.

"What did you do?" I said as I reached the driver's side door. "Tell me that wasn't some kind of forbidden spell."

"Get in!" Monty said, getting in and gesturing. "This should be enough...I hope."

"You *hope?*" I said, diving into the Dark Goat, slamming the door closed. "What exactly did you throw at the ogre?"

"It's an experimental variation," Monty said, still gesturing, as he finished casting. "I was able to analyze the runic nova you unleashed on the Sanctuary..."

"You unleashed a runic nova?" I said, whirling in my seat to see the oncoming ogre. "Are you insane?"

"Are you?" Monty said. "I would never unleash a runic nova in a city. No, this is my variation on the nova: an entropic siphon."

"That sounds dangerously close to a void vortex," I said, staring at the ogre, who had now stopped in its attack. "Tell me it's *not* a void vortex."

"I just did," Monty said. "I really hope Cecil made this

vehicle extra indestructible. I really wasn't expecting a Mantle of Discord; that will complicate matters."

"I'm not getting a lot of confidence from you regarding this experimental cast," I said, starting the engine and strapping in. "Why do you sound so nervous?"

"This is the first time I've used it," he said strapping in. "When the explosion starts, get out as fast as possible."

"Can you explain what this Mantle thing is and why it's a problem?"

"Later. Right now, we need to be prepared to move," Monty said, looking at the ogre. "When the siphon presents itself, we need to traverse the whirlwind, at speed. That should eject us at least fifty feet away, if my calculations are right—providing the runes on the vehicle hold."

"The what? Whirlwind? What was that about being ejected and runes holding?"

"The siphon will create a whirlwind of energy," Monty said, pointing at the ogre. "We need to go *into* the whirlwind fast and use its momentum to launch us to the other side. When we land, we need to be at least fifty feet away."

"And if we aren't?"

"Then we'll be too close, and it won't matter," Monty said. "It's starting."

The ogre stopped advancing and stood in the center of the alley, clawing at its chest where the two orbs had burrowed their way past the orange shield. It ripped pieces of its skin off in an attempt to get to the orbs, but failed, falling to its knees.

"I am the first of legion, Marked of Kali!"he screamed as a large violet-red orb began forming in his midsection. "You may have destroyed me, but we *will* find you. You... cannot...hide...from...us!"

"Now, Simon, now!"

I floored the gas and raced backward at the ogre, who exploded before I reached him. The next moment, a whirlwind of black-and-red energy formed where the ogre knelt.

"Monty, that looks like a tornado of death," I said. "Are you sure?"

"No, but we don't have a choice," he said, his eyes focused on the whirlwind. "Go through it and don't stop."

I kept my foot on the gas. Peaches whined as we got closer and Monty began gesturing as we sped into the tornado of destruction.

EIGHTEEN

When Cecil, the owner and head mad rune inscriber at SuNaTran, first expressed the desire that he wanted to find a way to destroy the Beast, Grey Sneaker's nightmare of a menace disguised as a car, he told us he runed the Dark Goat with the same runes found on the Beast.

I thought he was insane.

Creating two vehicles that are impossible to destroy, *and* have the potential to kill their drivers, sounds beyond homicidal. Right now, I was grateful that homicidal maniac was on our side.

I kept my foot on the gas as the Dark Goat punched into the whirlwind of energy with a screech and tearing of metal. We were lifted up and whipped around as parts of the Dark Goat were ripped off.

Peaches whined even louder as the driver's side mirror was sheared off. I saw one of the wheels bounce off the hood and slam into the windshield.

It was not looking good for the Dark Goat.

"Monty?" I said, white-knuckling the steering wheel as

the passenger-side mirror flew by. This was followed by small cracks forming in the driver's side window. "Did you just kill the Dark Goat?"

"Only if Cecil's runes fail us," Monty said, holding on to the door handle. "Brace yourself."

"For what?" I yelled. "What more can we possibly face?"

The interior of the Dark Goat took on a red glow, reminding me of the interior of a darkroom, back when photographic film was developed in fluid.

Peaches let out another whine mixed with a low growl as the red light became deeper and shifted to orange. I felt the pull of energy from my body as the Dark Goat reassembled itself.

We sailed out of the whirlwind and landed in the middle of 1st Avenue, bouncing forwards uncontrollably, narrowly missing several taxicabs before coming to a stop across the street.

Incredibly, the Dark Goat was intact.

I couldn't say the same for my nerves as I sat in the Dark Goat and looked across to the alley. The whirlwind had siphoned a large chunk of the alley into nothingness.

For a few seconds, I sat absolutely still, waiting for the world to catch up.

<You need practice. If you ate more meat, you would drive better.>

<Meat has nothing to do with what just happened.>

<I know. Meat would help you move the car straight, not in circles. Please eat more meat.>

I slowly exited the Dark Goat, unsteady on my feet.

I was about to respond to my very zen hellhound when Monty stepped out. I noticed he wasn't looking at the damage in the alley. I followed his gaze and saw the figure on the roof of the adjacent building; I couldn't tell much, except that it was a female and was glowing the same orange as the disassembled Ogre. She gave me a short nod and disappeared from sight.

"Who, or what, was that?"

"The next successor, obviously," Monty said. "I'm certain we'll find out who that is in short order."

"I'm not really up for another 'I'm going to eliminate you' session," I said, still looking up at the roof. "Can we put the assassins on hold until we deal with the *current* situation?"

"Would you like to contact Kali and explain how your new mark is inconveniencing you?" Monty asked. "I'm sure she'll be open to rearranging the attacks around a reasonable schedule. Perhaps mornings till noon and no weekends?"

"How many centuries will it take for me to get used to what you call humor?" I said, glancing at him. "She was glowing orange like the ogre. What does that mean?"

"The Mantle of Discord has been passed," Monty said, glancing at me. "How do you feel?"

"How do I feel? We just flew out of an alley via magical whirlwind in a car that can't be killed, after facing off against an ogre who wanted to erase me. How do you think I feel?"

"That is what occurred, but how do you *feel?*"

"Tired," I said, sitting behind the wheel. "Like I just ran ten blocks at top speed. I could take a solid nap right now."

"Not a luxury we can afford," Monty said, getting back into the Dark Goat. "The exhaustion you're feeling is the effect of the runes in the vehicle. It drew on your life force to reassemble itself."

"You're saying the Dark Goat is an energy vampire now? Because if that's the case, I'd like to return it to Cecil ASAP."

"Not an energy vampire, and Cecil doesn't do returns on vehicles like this," he said. "I'm certain Grey has tried to return his vehicle at some point."

"Hasn't worked out too well for him," I said. "Okay, not an energy vampire—then what?"

"More like a parasitic organism that will feed off your life force to maintain its integrity," Monty said, examining the interior of the Dark Goat. "I honestly didn't know if it would work. Cecil is a genius in his madness."

"Still sounds kind of vampirish. How long am I going to feel like this?"

"Should pass in a few minutes," he said. "I'm certain your curse should be working to undo any damage."

He was right. My body flushed hot and I began feeling better almost immediately.

"Do you know how often this is going to happen?" I said, touching the steering wheel warily in case the Dark Goat still felt hungry. "That draining was not fun."

"How often is what going to happen?" Monty said. "The vehicle being exploded while we're inside, or the draining of your life force?"

"Both?"

"My theory is that the two events are interrelated," he said. "If the vehicle senses its integrity is threatened, it will draw on you to power the runes Cecil inscribed."

"The last time it exploded it didn't do that."

"It must possess an internal power source it defaults to

if you aren't driving. It will draw on that first, unless you are in the driver's seat. Then it must be keyed to your signature, so that it can draw on your nearly-infinite supply of life energy."

"So…I'm a battery?"

"A very powerful battery," Monty said. "I'll have to ask Cecil for the details on the runes he used, but after the Midnight Ghost, he seems reluctant to answer my calls."

"Reluctant, really? That doesn't seem like Cecil."

"I was thinking the same thing," Monty said. "Usually he would take this moment to vent his frustration at the destruction."

"Could have something to do with you returning just the steering wheel of that piece of art," I said. "Maybe that's why he doesn't want to talk to you?"

"That wasn't me, that was Douglas," Monty said. "Besides, I did say I would commission another if that one was destroyed."

"He didn't lend the Duezy to Douglas, he lent it to *you* with specific instructions: don't blow it up, or something along those lines."

"To us," Monty clarified. "He lent it to *us*."

"Will you please stop with this 'us'? He gave it to *you*. He did seem proud of his work. Recreating that car must have cost a fortune and taken forever."

"I'll give him some space before calling again."

"I think Cecil just needs a grieving period," I said. "That automobile was an amazing piece of art. I'm sure he'll talk to you, eventually."

"Your creature performed superbly," Monty said, looking at my hellhound in the backseat. "You were a good boy."

Monty made a large sausage and fed it to my ever-willing hellhound, who inhaled the meat out of existence in a split-second.

<Please tell the angry man thank you.>

<Tell him yourself... On second thought, I'll tell him.>

"He says, thank you."

"He is very welcome. Thank you for showing restraint and not unleashing your magic missile."

"Why didn't you want me to use it?"

"The ogre was an audition," he said "Whoever sent him was gathering data on you and your capabilities."

"I could have probably blasted that glowgre to dust," I said. "My magic missile is fierce now. Wouldn't that have just scared everyone else away?"

"Possibly," Monty said, rubbing his chin. "Or they would have sent something even worse than an ogre. The ogre said they were legion. I don't know if that was boasting, but the less they know about your abilities, the better."

"Legion," I said. "This is getting biblical. Isn't a legion something like two thousand?"

"Close," Monty said. "A legion, biblical or Roman, consisted of four to six *thousand* members."

"Four to six thousand? This whole successor thing is going to keep happening, isn't it?"

Monty nodded.

"Even if the ogre was exaggerating, I'd have to agree that more of these 'successors' will be trying to kill you."

"There has to be some way to hide this mark," I said, tapping my forehead. "Or at the very least make it harder to detect."

"I don't know if I can mask the mark Kali gave you,"

he said, glancing my way. "I'd have to examine it closely, and we don't have that kind of time right now."

"So, in the meantime I'm going to get more successors trying to blast me to bits...How fun."

"It seems like it's only one at a time," Monty said. "At least that will make it manageable. As long as you aren't driving when you encounter the next bearer of the Mantle, you should avoid being drained or riding in an exploding car."

"Well, since you put it *that* way, how could I be upset at this new situation?" I said. "You mean I should embrace having an enormous target on me that attracts beings of utmost destruction?"

"Exactly," Monty said. "When life hands you lemons and all that."

"I'd like to avoid those scenarios in the future," I said, starting the engine again with a throaty rumble. I shook my head in amazement. "Cecil may be insane with his runes, but he's good at what he does. What about the big hole of nothing in the alley? Will someone walk into that and get hurt?"

"It will self-repair in an hour," Monty said, glancing across the street. "We need to get uptown. The next entrance for the Moving Market is at Carl Schurz Park in twenty minutes."

"How do you even know this?" I said. "Is there some kind of Moving Market entrance schedule somewhere I don't know about?"

"The Moving Market has a very particular energy signature if you know what to look for," Monty said. "It's almost like sensing the ripples of vibrations across a large field. Every time it moves—and it's on a fixed rotation, unlike, say, the Living Library—it sends out these runic vibrations."

"Still doesn't explain how you know it's going to be uptown in twenty minutes," I said, pulling into traffic and heading uptown. "That explanation just sounds like mages-peak. You could just say it's too complicated to explain. Is that so hard?"

"It *is* too complicated to explain in depth," Monty said. "But as a non-mage thrust into this world, it's important you have some idea of how things work. It could save our lives one day."

"I hope it never comes down to my knowledge to save us."

"Agreed," Monty said, leaning back in his seat and closing his eyes. "Let's go. The next entrance after Carl Schurz Park won't appear for a few hours. We don't have that kind of time."

"Got it," I said, stepping on the gas. "Let's get the etheric tightener."

NINETEEN

"Tether," Monty said when we arrived in front of the park on East End and 84th Street. "Not tightener. It's an etheric tether."

"Are you sure? It sounds more like a tightener to me."

"I'm certain, seeing as how I studied this, but please, illuminate me as to this tightener definition of yours. What exactly is an etheric tightener according to the Strong Dictionary of Magic?"

"The etheric tightener tightens our energy to this plane so the Soul Renderer can't rip our souls from our bodies. That about right?"

"Absolutely not," he said, opening his door. "An etheric tether maintains our connection to our life force when attacked."

"Right, tightening our energy to this plane."

"The tether prevents the Soul Renderer from casting a disintegration."

"Wait, what? He can disintegrate people? What the hell? You didn't say anything about being disintegrated."

"Dis-integrate in the true sense of the word," Monty clarified. "Not in the 'reducing you to your component atoms' sense, but rather disconnecting you from your source of energy. For a mage, or pretty much anyone, that usually proves fatal."

I opened the door for my sprawlific hellhound, who proceeded to exit the Dark Goat without so much as causing a bounce in the suspension.

Monty nodded in approval.

"That is quite impressive," he said. "This way. The entrance is close."

We entered the park and headed up the stairs to the promenade that looked over the East River. Next to the benches sat a small maintenance building.

Monty headed in that direction as I observed the early-afternoon park goers and wondered if they would notice two men and a hellhound entering a maintenance building.

"You don't think people will notice?" I said, still looking around. "We don't exactly look like we work for the Parks Department."

"Habituation," Monty said. "People stop noticing things they see or hear many times. We are currently operating under a minor illusion that allows the general populace to see what they expect to see."

"Do you know what they are seeing?"

"I would imagine two maintenance workers and a maintenance dog about to enter this building."

"Maintenance dog?" I said incredulously. "Really?"

"You've lived in this city all your life," Monty said, gesturing. "What won't New Yorkers ignore?"

"Pretty much everything unless it directly impacts

them...even then, they may not pay it any mind."

"Now imagine that predisposition with the help of a constant illusion."

"Point taken," I said with a nod. "Though I don't think that would work with explosions."

"Even illusions have their limits."

Monty placed his hand on the door. I sensed a trickle of energy flow. A bright white light flashed at the edges of the door for half a second. He turned the handle and motioned for me to enter.

I stepped in and found myself in a familiar, wide, brightly lit, empty hallway. In the center of the hallway, stood a man dressed in standard mageiform—upscale black suit, white shirt, and gray tie.

That's where the similarities ended.

His face was covered by a featureless white mask, giving off a serious Phantom of the Opera vibe. He held a silver, rune-covered six-foot staff in one hand, a short sword in the other. I noticed the bulge of the dual holsters under the jacket and remembered he carried hand cannons which were larger versions of Grim Whisper. Around him, softly glowing white orbs moved around his body in lazy orbits.

"Tell me we aren't walking into a fight with the Doorman Janus again," I said under my breath as we approached. "I'm really not in the mood and I need my coffee."

"It's Janus or the Doorman, not both," Monty said, keeping his voice low. "We should be able to meet with Tessa if my uncle smoothed things over."

"And if he didn't and Tessa feels like unleashing the Doorman?"

"Then your battle coffee will have to wait. Let me do the talking."

"You know," I said as we stepped closer, "maybe you can have Zegna design a special mage staff for you. Something upscale with extra runic power and classiness. Something fashionable for the discerning mage?"

"Mages do not use staves," Monty replied with a huff. "Now shut it. I don't think the Janus will appreciate your acerbic wit."

"It is shut," I said. "Let me know if you need me to bring the power."

Monty gave me a short glare and then focused on the Doorman.

"Mage Montague, you have requested access to the Moving Market," the Janus said, his voice reverberating in the hallway. "Identification, please."

"Of course." Monty stepped close and stared at the mask. A golden light emanated the Janus' eyes and he nodded. "Tristan Montague, Mage of the Golden Circle. Identification confirmed. You may proceed."

I made to walk forward and follow Monty when the Doorman blocked the hallway with his staff.

"Marked of Kali," the Doorman said in a voice which sounded like several people speaking at once, not at all like the voice he used for Monty. "Identify yourself."

"You just said who I was," I replied, surprised. "It's not like I carry my 'Marked of Kali' ID on me."

"This is most irregular," Monty said. "Are you certain this is required?"

"Marked of Kali, identify yourself," the Doorman repeated, ignoring Monty. "Authorization is required. Failure to comply will result in your dismissal."

"He says dismissal, but it sounds like he means termination," I said, keeping my distance. "Is he serious? Last time, I was able to go through as your guest."

I stared at Monty, who motioned for me to step closer to the Doorman.

"He needs to scan your face and runic signature," Monty said. "Step closer."

"Can't he do that from there?" I said, staring at the impassive mask of the Doorman. "I'd rather not get within the reach of his staff. I've been *Yat-thwacked* enough the last few days."

"What makes you think you aren't in reach of it now?"

"If he attacks me, it's your fault."

"He's not going to attack you, unless you fail to follow his instructions. Identify yourself."

I stepped forward, keeping one eye on the location of the silver staff. This one was longer than Master Yat's and covered in dangerous, nasty-looking runes. I was certain getting *thwacked* by it wasn't just going to be a matter of pain and a bruise.

I stepped close and stared at the mask. A golden light emanated from his eyes as the Doorman nodded.

"Marked of Kali, Shield-warrior to Mage Montague, Aspis of Kali, and bondmate to this hellhound"—he motioned to Peaches with the staff—"identification confirmed. You may proceed."

I stepped a little closer.

"Hey, DJ," I said with a nod. "Are you going to try and blast us like the last time we were here?"

"Simon, don't antagonize the Janus. He was doing what he was instructed to do. He serves the Moving Market, and by default, Tessa."

"Just making sure," I said, walking past the Doorman. "Last time he was acting like a real Janus without the J."

Monty shook his head as we headed down the hallway.

"The identification protocol was unexpected," he said as we came to a large door. "Remember, no matter what my uncle may have said or arranged, the Moving Market is hostile territory. Treat it as such."

"I'll remember to shoot first and forget the questions if things go sideways," I said with a nod. "How did he know I'm your Shield-warrior and an Aspis?"

"They are one and the same," Monty said. "It would seem that whatever upgrade Kali performed on you, has increased your reputation. Normally I would say it's flattering, but in these cases, the more you are known, the shorter your life expectancy."

"Wonderful," I said. "Something else to thank Kali for. It's almost like she's trying to get me killed."

"She probably is," Monty said. "She is not your friend and never will be. Always keep that present in your mind. She is an ancient goddess of death who wields almost immeasurable power. To her, you are less than an afterthought, if she gives you thought at all."

"Way to boost the morale," I said. "From now on, I'm just going to call you Motivational Monty: Crusher of Spirits, Destroyer of Hope, and Master of Bleakness."

"I'd rather you didn't, thank you," he said pointing at the door. "Through here."

"This feels like a horrible idea."

"It is, but it's the only one we have," Monty said, opening the door. "Let's make this meeting as brief as possible."

TWENTY

We stood in Market Central.

They had made significant changes since the last time I was here. We had created a trail of destruction—and no, it wasn't our fault. Well, mostly not our fault. Roque had run rampant on the seventh ring during our last visit.

The last time I saw him he was about to face off against the Doorman. It was a testament to the Doorman's power that he was able to face a dragon in dragon form and walk away unscathed. I really hoped Dex had moved Roque someplace safe—maybe a cave on a tropical island with ample room for a hoard of gold, or whatever passed for dragon luxury.

I could see several alterations had been made, but the original design remained mostly unchanged. The entire market was still arranged like a wheel formed of seven concentric circles.

This building, which also doubled as the main base of operations, acted as the hub of the wheel. The rings were arranged in order of influence and power.

The higher-ranked magic-users inhabited the rings closest to the hub. The two outer rings were a dead zone. If you found yourself on an outer ring, it was only a matter of time before someone or something tried to introduce you to the concept of the dead zone—emphasis on dead.

There was one law in the Market: only the strong, cunning, or ruthless survived for any length of time. The last time I had stood in this reception area, I had recently lost Peaches, and was feeling particularly homicidal at the time.

Now, I was acutely aware we were in a no-man's land of sorts. We stood in a large reception area that resembled the lobby of a large hotel. Some of the patrons seated around the space gave us openly hostile looks.

"Seems like the stink eyes followed us from Ezra's," I said, glancing around. "You'd think Tessa doesn't like us or something."

"She doesn't," Monty said, taking a seat in the reception area. Several of the patrons seated near us subsequently stood and relocated to the other side. "She may have to accept us because of my uncle, but remember that she is not bound to treat us well—just civilly."

"I'm guessing that treatment doesn't extend to anyone else in the Moving Market," I said, taking a seat next to Monty as Peaches parked by my feet in ready-to-pounce-and-shred mode. "I'm getting serious 'I hate you' vibes in here."

"Those in the hub will manage their dislike," Monty said, ignoring the looks. "I don't think a trip to the outer rings would be prudent. If something occurs out there, Tessa can claim plausible deniability to my uncle or anyone else who will inquire why we were attacked."

"Right. Stay in the hub, get the tether, and get the hell out of Dodge."

"That's it in a nutshell," Monty said glancing around. "She should see us soon."

"Or she can have these lovely guests come together and try and wipe us out," I said, noticing some of the glares were harder than others. "Seriously, what did your uncle say to her?"

"Oh, I doubt most of this is my uncle's doing," Monty said, raising a hand and motioning to the young woman who was headed our way. "I would hazard that most of the animosity you are experiencing is due to your mark."

A statuesque woman holding a clipboard approached us. She was dressed in a sharp, dark-blue business suit and her name-tag read 'Anna'.

"Welcome, Mage Montague," Anna said, and then turned to me. "Mr. Strong. This way, please. Ms. Wract is waiting for you."

"What happened to Kathy?" I said as we stood and followed Anna across the reception floor. "She was here the last time we visited."

"Kathy was terminated," Anna said icily. "She failed to perform her duties to the standard of the Market."

This time I knew *terminated* either meant relocated to the outer rings, or Kathy had been fired permanently... from life.

Anna led us to the other end of the reception area.

The space was done in minimalist art deco, with plenty of wood and stone surrounding the open area in the center. The subtle smell of citrus and fresh earth made me pause for a second, until I noticed the vases filled with flowers on several of the wall stands.

Standing alone on the far side of the reception area stood Tessa. She nodded when she saw us, and smiled. In that moment, I realized how dangerous Tessa was. I remembered Monty's description of her abilities: *She's a Time Weaver. She keeps the Moving Market...moving. Not only does she slip it in between planes, she's also powerful enough to move it through time.*

She put down a tablet she was using and motioned for Anna to approach. Tessa wore a slate-gray Armani pantsuit, which complemented her white hair and exuded unspoken power—both the illusion of it, and the real energy she controlled around her.

Her presence was undiminished from the last time we met. She commanded the attention of those around her with a sense of ease and a not-so-subtle undercurrent of menace.

Tessa owned the Market, and she knew it.

She gave us another pleasant smile, and I remembered Monty's words: *Even sharks smile before they rip you to shreds.* Her piercing hazel eyes shimmered with violet power as we approached with Anna in the lead.

"Mage Montague, Mr. Strong, " she said, her words warm and affectionate, setting off even more alarms in my head. "It *is* good to see you both again."

I'm sure she meant to add the word...*alive*. Especially after setting the Doorman and her guard dragon on us during our last visit.

"The feeling is mutual," Monty said, flexing the diplomacy. "It appears the last time we were here, we allowed a difference of opinion to come between us. I hope we can reconcile that misunderstanding."

The difference of opinion was clear. We enjoyed breathing and

Tessa wanted us to stop. I managed to keep my thoughts to myself, at least for now.

"Of course we can," she said, looking at Anna. "We'll be in my office. Hold all my calls."

"Yes, ma'am. Would your guests like anything to drink?"

"Earl Grey steeped to perfection for Mr. Montague," Tessa said. "Coffee, extra black, no sugar for Mr. Strong."

"Right away, ma'am," Anna said, gliding away.

"She seems nice," I said, watching Anna walking away. "Real go-getter."

"I don't employ people based on how nice they are, Mr. Strong," Tessa answered with a smile that never reached her eyes. "I employ people who are relentless in the pursuit of perfection. That is what the Market stands for."

"Oh, I thought the Market stood for facilitating the procurement of goods most considered bann—rare and hard to find?"

Her smile was positively predatory, but I was enjoying my diplomacy too much to take notice. Mages weren't the only ones who could say what needed to be said under the disguise of tact.

"We *are* a market for the rare and difficult to find, yes, among other things. We also cater to those select clientele with discerning taste, such as yourselves."

I was feeling downright twitchy, but I didn't want to ruin Monty's amazing moment of diplomacy. I made sure to keep my hand away from Grim Whisper.

Tessa placed a hand on the wall near us. A section of the wall slid back silently, giving us access to her office.

Tessa's office was a large, expansive area. Neat stacks of paper covered her behemoth Parnian desk, and set in front of it were two large leather chairs. The walls were bare, except for a large reproduction of Dali's *Galatea of the Spheres*. A smaller version of *The Persistence of Memory* sat on her desk.

"I see you changed the Dali," I said, examining the art on the wall. "Another original?"

"Yes," Tessa said, taking a seat behind her desk. "Gala was Dali's inspiration. I thought it only fitting to have this piece here. She was gracious enough to gift it to me. Courtesy of Salva, of course."

"Of course," I said. "It's amazing."

"Thank you. Please, sit," she said, motioning to the chairs in front of her desk. "I would like to know what spurred you to grace the Market with your presence again."

Unspoken in that last comment was the implicit meaning: *How dare you come back here after I tried to kill you last time?*

I sat in one of the two Gio Ponti 1950s armchairs facing her. Monty sat in the other. Tessa was many things, but she had taste when it came to furniture and clothing. Everything else about her made me want to put a few entropy rounds in her, but I figured Monty would be upset at that reaction.

Next to the enormity of her desk stood Eileen, Tessa's personal assistant. She wore a black pantsuit almost identical to Tessa's. She held a large tablet and wore an earpiece, tapping it a few times as we sat.

"You remember Eileen, my personal assistant," Tessa said, motioning to the woman. "She will be taking your requisition." She sat back and gazed at Monty. "Which is?"

"We need an etheric tether," Monty said. "One we can key to multiple signatures."

"Eileen?" Tessa asked, without taking her eyes off of us. "Availability?"

Eileen tapped the tablet a few times and showed the results to Tessa, who frowned before nodding.

"Is that the only location?"

Eileen nodded.

"Yes, ma'am," Eileen said. "They are too volatile to keep in the inner rings."

I didn't like where the conversation was going.

"Are you certain you need an etheric tether?" Tessa said, placing both hands on her desk and looking at us with a look of concern. "Would it be possible to substitute the item for one of a similar purpose?"

"I'm afraid not," Monty said. "We will be dealing with a specific catalyst. The etheric tether will ensure our interaction results in a positive outcome."

"I see," Tessa said, steepling her fingers. "An etheric tether means you are facing a serious catalyst. If you need one that can be keyed to various signatures, I'm afraid the only ones I can offer you are located on the outer ring. The outermost ring, to be precise."

"What a surprise," I said, barely holding back the contempt. "I'm sure the odds of that happening are astronomical."

"What are you trying to imply, Mr. Strong?"

"I'm not *trying* to imply anything," I said. "I'm calling it like it is. So let's cut the shit. *You* don't like us, and *we* certainly don't like you. This pretense is bullshit. If you could, you'd dust us right now."

"Who says I can't?" Tessa said, raising an eyebrow.

"Removing you in the Market, *my* Market, would be a simple exercise. People disappear here all the time."

"I don't think so," I said, pushing it. "If it was so simple, we wouldn't be breathing right now, would we?"

Tessa nodded and smiled again, sending shivers through me. This was like playing with fire while being doused in gasoline. I may have been outclassed in the power department, but she was going to know we didn't fear her.

"True," she said. "Removing you here, now, would result in...complications. It would cause a disruption I'm not prepared to deal with at the moment. But make no mistake: you are not welcome here...ever. Understood?"

"Understood," Monty said. "Where is the tether?"

"Do you need to ask?" I said. "I have a pretty good guess on which ring its located. Seven?"

"Ring seven," Tessa confirmed and stared at Monty. "Who do you have as next of kin? Dexter?"

"That won't be necessary," Monty said. "Where in the seventh ring?"

"Northern edge. You will need to meet a vendor named Stark," Tessa said. "I want to take this moment to ask you to reconsider. The outer rings are lawless areas. They are dangerous, and even with your combined abilities, I cannot guarantee your safety."

"Thank you for the warning," Monty said. "What payment will this vendor require and where on the northern edge?"

"He is the only Master Artificer in the Market," she said. "He guards his privacy violently."

"How violently? Asking for a friend."

"*If* you manage to get past his defenses and reach him

alive, I will cover the cost of the tether," Tessa added. "It's the least I can do in the spirit of cooperation and reconciliation."

"Someone acting in the spirit of cooperation and reconciliation would ship the tether here and deliver it to us," I said. "You know, seeing as how the outer rings are *so* dangerous."

Tessa smiled, and violet energy raced across her eyes. It was the kind of smile that made you reconsider poking the angry bear you happened to bump into while taking a walk in the forest at night.

As Monty would say, in for a penny, in for a pound. There was no turning back now, and I had no illusions that whatever was waiting for us in the seventh ring wasn't going to try and end us, with extreme violence.

"I'm afraid I'm constrained by the regulations of my position," Tessa said. "The Moving Market is just that, a market. We, as an entity, do not cater to individual requests. We provide the access and information on where to find the desired item a client requires, but it would infringe on the free-market system that sustains us if we were to provide an individualized delivery service. I'm sure you understand."

"I understand," I said. "You want us to do our dying in the dangerous and lawless seventh ring where you can say you had nothing to do with it."

"We *understand*," Monty said, glaring at me and getting to his feet. "I would appreciate it if Stark could be informed of our impending arrival. Thank you, again."

"Eileen will let him know," Tessa said, standing. "It has been my pleasure being of service to you. Pass on my regards to your uncle. Safe travels."

"Are you going to let the Ringrail know we're going to the outer ring?" I said. "You know, to ensure our *safe* travels?"

"I'm afraid the Ringrail is currently under construction to the outer rings and inaccessible due to some recent tunnel collapses," Tessa said, looking at me. "For your safety, I have provided a more *direct* route."

"A more direct route, really?" I said. "Is the Doorman going to be escorting us along this direct route?"

"The Doorman will escort you to the entrance. Sadly, he will be otherwise occupied, and will not accompany you to the outer ring. I'm sure you understand."

"I do," I said, standing as well. "Where I come from, we call that 'plausible deniability'."

"Your frankness is refreshing, Mr. Strong, but I can assure you, whatever outcome befalls you, if it happens in my Market, I am responsible," she said. "You would do well to bear that in mind."

"I will, and I do," I said, with restrained menace. "I think, some time in the future, the Moving Market will have to change its management. I really hope you survive the restructuring."

"Your concern is flattering, but unneeded. I have survived things you could not imagine. No one would dare attack me in the Market," she said, her voice matching the menace in mine. "I'm confident that you both have the wherewithal to keep yourselves safe as you venture to the outer rings." She turned to Eileen. "Please see them out."

Eileen escorted us out of Tessa's office and back into the reception area.

TWENTY-ONE

"I didn't even get my coffee," I said as we stood in the reception area. "I'd like to file a formal complaint."

"It will have to wait, I think."

"That is the height of bad manners," I said, offended. "How do you offer someone coffee and fail to deliver? This...is...coffee we're talking about here. It's just not done."

"It may have had something to do with the fact you were overtly accusing her of trying to kill us," Monty said, glancing around the reception area. "Most megalomaniacs consider themselves to be benign caretakers of those under their power."

"I still think Dex should've just blasted her to little Tessa bits."

"That would have created a power vacuum in the Market," Monty said. "If he had, he'd have to install the next Director of the Market, something I'm sure my uncle considered when he spoke with her last."

"Knowing Dex, it would be the last thing he would

want to do," I said. "So, for now, we deal with the devil we know who is actively trying to end us."

"That actually went better than expected," Monty said. "My uncle must have had some strong words with Tessa."

"I wouldn't want a pissed-off Dex coming for me either," I said with a shudder. "What were you expecting, actually?"

"I was expecting we'd be fighting our way out of the Market."

"The day is still young," I said, looking around at the hostile glances we were getting. "We may still have to."

The Doorman approached us.

"This way, please," he said. "I've been instructed to escort you out of this ring."

"I'm feeling safer already, DJ," I said as we followed him down several corridors away from the reception area. Peaches rumbled by my side as we entered a mid-sized room empty of all furniture.

I immediately felt the temperature drop.

Every surface in this room was rune-covered gray marble. On the far side, opposite the entrance, I saw seven steel doors. The room itself felt colder than the reception area, and I could see my exhalation on every breath.

<This place is bad. It feels bad.>

<What are you feeling? Why is it bad?>

<It smells bad. There is something bad here.>

<We'll be careful. Let me know if you sense anything else.>

<I sense hunger. I am so hungry.>

<Anything else that could hurt us.>

<Not having meat can hurt my stomach.>

<Anything else besides the lack of meat in your stomach.>

"My hound gave this place a nose down," I said under my breath to Monty. "Heads up on unfriendlies."

"The entire Market is unfriendly," Monty replied. "A little more specificity would be appreciated."

"Not big on specifics, just not a good vibe," I said, taking in the room. "I'm going to have to agree with him on this one. This room is creeping me out."

The Doorman stood next to one of the doors. I counted the sequence and realized he was standing next to the seventh door counting from left to right. Out of the seven doors, only the sixth and seventh were heavily runed. The seventh contained the most, along with some major "open me and die" vibes coming off the door in waves.

"This is the door you will require," Doorman said. "You will have to find alternative methods of egress. These portals only allow for outward travel to the rings."

"Outward travel only?" I said. "So we can check out any time we want, but we can never leave?"

I figured, being in the Moving Market all the time, he'd never get the reference.

"Outward travel only," Doorman said with a nod. "The denizens of the seventh ring are prisoners of their own device. The Director has forbidden travel inward from the outer rings."

My mouth dropped as the Doorman turned and faced the door. I turned to Monty, who was oblivious, and focused on the door. More specifically, the nasty-looking lethal runes inscribed on the door.

The steel door was covered in red warning runes. No one opened this door by accident, and if they did, the runes I could make out explained how it would be the last door they ever opened while breathing.

DJ placed his hand on the door, and the runes switched from red to blue. He pulled on the handle, opened the door, and motioned for us to continue. I peeked past the Doorman and saw another corridor. The secondary corridor looked about as inviting as a minefield.

"Sure you don't want to, you know...lead the way?" I said, looking at the Doorman. "You know, to make sure we make it safely to the other side?"

"Your safety is not my concern," the Doorman said. "I have been tasked with opening this portal and showing you the way. My responsibilities end there. If you wish to deviate from this course of action, I have been instructed to deter you...with force, if necessary."

"So, basically, go through the door or pain."

The Doorman nodded.

"Your choice," he said. "This is the only way to the seventh ring and the item you seek."

"How badly do we need this tether?" I said, turning to Monty. "Can we face the Soul Shredder without it?"

"Yes, but it would be akin to walking through a hail of gunfire without a bulletproof vest, while stopping to read the Sunday paper mid-stroll," Monty said, looking into the second corridor. "Highly inadvisable."

"Fine, if you're going through hell, keep going," I said, resigned to the possibility of dying or at the very least feeling extreme pain in the next corridor. "Do you see any traps or defenses?"

"I'm not worried about the defenses I can see," Monty said, gesturing. "It's the ones I may miss that concern me."

White runes floated down the corridor as Monty stepped in. I turned to the Doorman one more time.

"You may want to consider a career change," I said, glancing at Monty, who was slowly making his way forward. "Your boss sucks, and if you keep working for her, it means you agree with the shit she spreads in the Market."

The Doorman looked at me, and for a brief moment I thought I saw a flicker of regret.

"I serve the Market, not the Director," he said. "That is my purpose as gatekeeper and always will be. Do you know your purpose?"

"I do," I said, stepping into the corridor after Monty with Peaches in tow. "My purpose is to make sure people like your boss are stopped."

"Then your purpose is doomed. There will always be people like the Director."

"Which means there will always be people like me to stop people like her," I said. "Even if I fail, I'm going down swinging."

"Yet, you are still going down. Good luck in the seventh ring. Look to the shadows and avoid the Unbound...if you can."

I was about to ask what he meant when he closed the door in my face. The next second, the door I had stepped through was gone. I caught up with Monty a few seconds later, who was continuing to proceed slowly down the corridor.

Every few steps he would release more runes, which would float on ahead of us, disappearing in the walls and floor. I had a feeling he was doing some kind of runic mine detecting.

"DJ said something peculiar just now," I said as Monty kept gesturing. "It was unexpected."

"More unexpected than knowing the song you referred to?" Monty said without looking at me. "The Janus are vast repositories of knowledge as well as gatekeepers. In history, they were known to allow passage only if a series of riddles was answered correctly."

"What if they were answered incorrectly?"

"The person trying to obtain passage was usually dispatched," Monty said, sending another group of runes floating ahead of us. "What did he say?"

"Look to the shadows and avoid the Unbound...if you can."

Monty stopped walking.

"Are you certain?" he said, looking back the way we came. "Those were his exact words?"

"He just said them a few seconds ago," I said. "Yes, I'm sure."

"That...is bad."

"Excuse me? What part of this whole visit is good?"

"You don't understand," Monty said, looking around. "The Doorman was warning us as best he could."

"Warning us? Warning us against what? Why would he warn us?"

"An excellent question I have no answer for," Monty said, moving forward. "As for what he's warning us against...the Unbound."

"The Unbound? But that would mean...?"

"The seventh ring is a trap," Monty finished. "We have only one way to go now."

"Can't you create a teleportation circle or something? A portal we can use to bypass this trap and get the tether?"

"No. Tessa has reconfigured the Market," Monty said, shaking his head. "Perhaps my uncle could pull off a circle in here, but my ability is nowhere near his. No teleportation circles."

"Wait—maybe my hellhound can planewalk us out?"

"Even if he could, which I doubt, he could only take us out of the entire Market," Monty said. "We need to get to the seventh ring. Exiting the Market would defeat the purpose of this entire exercise."

"Let me ask him anyway."

"Of course, humor yourself. You can even tell him I'll make him an extra-large sausage, only if he can pull it off."

Peaches' head turned at the words "extra-large sausage" as he fixed his gaze on Monty.

<Hey, boy. Do you think you can get us out of here? You know the way you do?>

<He said extra-large sausage.>

<Yes, he did, but before you focus on the priority of your life, can you try and see if you can get out of here?>

Peaches rumbled and chuffed.

<I can't. Everything is closed. I told you this place was bad.>

<Closed? What does that mean, closed?>

<When something is not open, it is closed. In here, I can't. All the ways are closed.>

<If that changes, can you let me know right away?>

<Is he still making the extra-large sausage?>

<Maybe later once we get out of here. I'll ask him. Remember, let me know if the ways open.>

Peaches chuffed again.

"He says everything is closed," I said, crouching down and rubbing my hellhound's massive head. "But he will stay alert and let me know as soon as that changes. Won't you, boy?"

Peaches nudged his head into my hand for more rubs as I stood.

"I'm not surprised," Monty said. "It seems we've been maneuvered here for a confrontation."

"Are you saying this was a setup?"

"Indeed," Monty said as we stood next to the door leading into the seventh ring proper. "Someone, my guess is Mahnes, knew we would come to the Market in search of a tether."

"How could he possibly know that? Besides, how hard is it to find these tethers?"

"It's what I would do," Monty said after a pause. "He's a mage, after all. I've been bloody stupid. How could I not see it?"

"See what?"

"The most effective way to combat a Soul Renderer—actually, the only way that has some measure of survivability when facing a Soul Renderer—is to employ a tether," Monty said, dropping into university-professor mode. "The only place to reliably get one is here, the Moving Market. It was a simple matter of leaving behind enough clues to position us here."

"Enough bodies, you mean," I said my voice grim. "Mahnes, or whoever this Renderer really is, killed an entire hub of NYTF personnel to send us a message."

"Ramirez didn't survive by his wits," Monty added. "That was intentional."

"Shit," I said, seeing the pieces and putting it together. "But they nearly killed him. Are you saying they let Ramirez live to deliver the message?"

"Yes," Monty said, gesturing again. "This kind of planning denotes a particular type of cunning."

"That explains getting us here," I said. "It doesn't explain what's waiting for us on the other side of this door. Why are there Unbound in the Market? Somehow they don't strike me as Moving Market shoppers."

"They aren't," Monty said. "Remember what the Doorman said: *Look to the shadows and avoid the Unbound…if you can.* Mahnes is waiting for us. Once we enter the seventh ring, he will send the Unbound."

"That gives us a window," I said, running rough calculations in my head. "How long before he knows we're on the seventh ring?"

"I'd say as soon as Tessa informs him," Monty said. "*Look to the shadows*…He must be using shadowports to send in the Unbound."

"Shadowports? Why does that sound like a bad thing?"

"Any shadow can be used as an entryway if he's using shadowports," Monty said. "We can do this. All we need to do is maintain a constant source of light and get past Stark's defenses."

"Somehow I don't recall the seventh ring being a place of sunshine and light," I said. "Dark, depressing, and deadly was more of the tone it was going for last time we were here."

"Be that as it may, we will have a small window of time before we can expect the Unbound," Monty said. "An artificer trying to hide will have a distinct energy signature."

"How is he hiding if he has a distinct energy signature? Doesn't that defeat the purpose of trying to hide?"

"Exactly," Monty said, making no sense. "We have to look for what's not there."

"Right," I said slowly. "Look for what's not there, of course."

"Ready?" Monty said, grabbing the handle of the door. "Once this door is opened, I'm certain Tessa will know our immediate location and notify Mahnes."

"So all we need to do is keep the place lit, evade the Unbound, and get past the Artificial's defenses? How hard could it be?"

"Artificer, and yes," Monty said reassuringly. "Not difficult at all."

"We are men of action. Lies do not become us," I said with a slight smile. "Admit it: this is going to be suicidal."

"Or close to it," Monty admitted. "I have every confidence in you."

He pulled open the door.

TWENTY-TWO

The seventh ring was similar to entering the wrong neighborhood at night wearing a neon sign that said ATTACK ME blinking bright red every few seconds.

The streets were dirty, the buildings were dirty, and the air was rancid. After a few seconds, even I felt grimy. Peaches rumbled his displeasure next to my leg as we walked down the street. I turned back to look at the door we had used, but it was gone.

Monty gestured and several large orbs of white light floated near us. It suddenly struck me that if Monty created a light, the immediate side effect of that action would be to create shadows.

"Monty?" I said, looking at the orbs circling above and around us. "These orbs of yours are fairly bright. Aren't they creating shadows?"

"Yes," Monty said with a nod. "Quite astute of you. However, they aren't static. The constant motion makes it impossible to use the shadows around us as ports, because the shadows are constantly in flux, shifting, changing both shape and location."

"So Mahnes can't use these shadows, but what about the shadows farther away?"

"That's what our weapons are for."

"Feeling much better now, thanks," I said. "Where exactly are we?"

"This is, according to my calculations, the northern edge," Monty said, looking around. "Stark should have his shop somewhere on this street."

I looked up and down the street. All of the shops looked similar: old and rundown. I couldn't even tell if it was morning, afternoon, or evening. The light of the sky was perpetually stuck at Night of the Living Dead intensity and pulsed with deep violet undertones against a backdrop of black and gray.

"Does it ever become day in the seventh ring?" I asked, examining the shops more closely. "This darkness isn't exactly giving me 'let's go out and shop' feels."

"This is daytime in the seventh ring," Monty said. "Here, quickly."

Monty stood in front of a storefront that read DESO-LATE CRAFTS which looked like it was used to test the explosive potential of C4 on a repeated basis. The window was blasted out, and to say the interior was destroyed, was actually paying the place a compliment.

"I'm going to go with the name fits the shop," I said, looking up at the sign above the window. "Emphasis on the desolate part."

"It's clever," Monty said, running his hands along the outer walls of the storefront. "It should be here somewhere."

"What should be here?" I said, examining the blown out storefront. "This looks like the Randy Rump after one of your renovations. It's completely destroyed, and I'm not getting any energy signatures."

"Yes. Exactly," Monty said, as the sound of hissing filled the street. "Mahnes knows we're here."

"What gave it away?" I said, drawing Grim Whisper. "That could just be a serious leakage of air somewhere."

"Of course," Monty said, stepping closer to the blasted out window. "Whatever you do, don't use your blade. If you siphon an Unbound, the results would be...unpleasant."

"Unpleasant? Which means *what* exactly?"

"The Unbound will try to imprint itself on you," Monty said. "You will end up with fragments of memories of those who were unbound. End up with enough of those and you will be driven mad."

"Right, keep blade away from Unbound, got it," I said. "Entropy rounds?"

"Don't know," Monty said, distracted, as he continued examining the outer walls of the shop. "I'd stick to your Dawnward and magic missile. Those *should* work."

"Should work?"

"I've never had the opportunity to face Unbound, Simon," Monty said. "I need to focus here. The theory is sound, however; your magic missile has basically an unlimited supply of power, and your Dawnward should keep them away."

"If I can form it," I said, looking around. "It hasn't exactly been reliable."

"There is that," Monty said, crouching down. "Don't

forget your creature. He may be able to stop them on his own—or at least the first hundred or so."

"The first hundred? How many of these things usually attack at once?"

"According to my studies, they usually appear in groups of four to five centuria."

"Four to five hundred? Are you shitting me?"

"Give or take a centuria," Monty said, tracing some runes and whispering words under his breath. "We can discuss Unbound numbers, *or* you can let me focus on deciphering these runes so we can get off this street."

"Off the street sounds great," I said. "I like that plan."

"Excellent," Monty said as a string of golden runes appeared in the wall in front of him. "Interesting. This appears to be the main defense and entrance."

"Sounds good," I said. "Do your finger wiggle, move the runes around, and let's get inside."

"It doesn't appear to be that simple. It's a question."

"A question of what? Are your fingers cramped? Let's get with the wiggling."

"I'm curious, how good are you at riddles?"

"Riddles? You're asking me about riddles now when we're about to be overrun with Unbound?"

"Our lives may depend on your answer, so yes—because according to this, if I answer it incorrectly, the Unbound will be the least of our worries."

"Okay then, no pressure," I said as the hissing got louder. "What's the riddle? And make it fast, because they're nearly here."

"This thing all things devours," Monty started as he read the runes on the wall. "Birds, beasts, trees, flowers; gnaws iron, bites steel; grinds hard stones to meal; slays kings, ruins town, and beats mountains down. What is it?"

"How am I supposed to know what it is? Some kind of super creature we haven't met yet?"

"The answer eludes me," Monty said, tapping his chin in frustration. "Its origin is not Persian, Celtic, Sumerian, or ancient Egyptian."

"Are you serious?" I said as I saw figures flit between buildings. "You're the mage!"

"Riddles were never my strong point," Monty said. "I should have devoted more study to them, but battle magic called. Who has the inclination to learn riddles when you can manipulate orbs of pure energy?"

"I get that you feel bad about this," I said, without taking my eyes off the street in front of me. "Really, I do, but we don't have time for regrets—the Unbound are incoming. Maybe you can ask them as they shred us?"

"Exactly!" Monty said, tracing a rune in the air. "That's it. How did I miss that?"

"You're welcome, I think?" I said, confused. "If you're going to do something, this would be the time."

"No one likes a show off, Simon," Monty said. "You've answered it. No need to rub it in."

"If I knew what you were talking about it, I'd rub it in," I said. "I don't. Can you open the door or get access or whatever to get off the street?"

"I'm on it," Monty said tracing one more rune. "There! That should do it."

The façade of the storefront melted away, exposing a large, wooden, rune-covered door. The runes flared as Monty pushed the door open, revealing a staircase leading upward.

"Inside! Now!" Monty said. "This will only remain open for a few seconds longer."

I raced in behind Monty with Peaches at my side. The hissing outside faded to silence as the door closed behind us.

TWENTY-THREE

Desolate Crafts turned out to be a quiet shop that resembled a combination of my high-school chemistry class mixed with wood and metal shops. I saw beakers and burners on several tables, next to drills, presses, brakes, and assorted machines designed to work both wood and metal.

Next to these, I saw other types of machines I didn't recognize, but I could tell they were used in some kind of metalworking. The whole place was a mash up of several disciplines all in one place. On the far side of the room, one of the walls was covered in books whose titles were indecipherable to me.

From the amount of items everywhere, I could tell it was a working shop.

The place was full without being messy. Most of the projects were in different stages of completion and I made sure not to touch anything. The runes I could understand on some of the items suggested that manipulating some of them would be the worst idea ever.

As scary as some of the runes read, the place felt strange and empty, as if the energy had been sucked out of it. A doorway led off to what I could only assume were living quarters of some kind.

"What is this place?" I asked, looking around. "This is like some kind of mad scientist's lab, but it feels off somehow, like it's missing *umph* or power. Everything seems stuck."

"*Umph?*" Monty said. "Your eloquence is staggering."

"I try," I said with a smirk. "If you study hard, one day you too can achieve my level of word mastery. Do you feel what I'm talking about, though?"

"No," Monty said, still looking around. "The fact that you can sense the absence of energy in this space means your sensitivity is growing. What's disturbing is that *I* don't sense this lack of *umph* you're referring to."

"So this isn't a mad scientist's lab, but more like a retired mage's lab?"

"Not too far off," Monty said, moving to the side of the room where the books were. "Some of these books were thought to have been lost. I can't believe he has a copy of Ziller's *Permutations*," he said, turning to face me. "This volume can actually teach you how to turn lead to gold and, more importantly, how diamonds can be created from any stone, not just coal."

"I see you've done your homework," a rough voice said from the doorway. "How did you get in here?"

Stark was average in height, with dark hair and a piercing stare. His goatee was flecked with gray and he looked semi-fit. He wore a pair of half-lens glasses and carried a large book in one hand. His other hand held a dangerous-looking...I wanted to say gun of some kind, but I wasn't sure.

"Well met, Master Artificer Stark," Monty said with a slight nod. "It's a pleasure to make your acquaintance."

"We'll see about that," Stark said, his gruff voice filling the shop. "The name's just Stark. I left all of that 'Master Artificer' puffery when I ended up here. You still didn't answer my question. How did you get in?"

"The front door?" I said. "I mean, after Monty figured out your riddle, that is."

Stark turned to Monty.

"You figured it out? Dammit! It was supposed to keep you out. Clearly my riddles are too easy."

"Actually, it was Simon who figured it out," Monty said, pointing at me. "I just implemented the inverse order application. Quite clever, actually."

"Obviously not clever enough, since you're standing in the middle of my shop, not on the street being shunted to another part of this ring," Stark said, glancing at me. "It was supposed to keep you out." He mumbled a few words under his breath."This is bad. You don't understand. You shouldn't be here. Not in here with me."

I gave Monty a look that said: *I think the retired mage is closer to mad scientist, emphasis on mad.*

Monty glared at me, and shook his head, warning me with a look that replied: *Do not say anything to set him off. He seems unstable as it is.*

"Why shouldn't we be here?" Monty said gently. "You are the Artificer, are you not?"

"*You* figured it out?" Stark said, giving me the once over as he ignored Monty. "You don't strike me as overly knowledgeable about the arcane. How did *you* figure it out?"

"I don't know," I said mildly insulted. "Ask him." I nodded my head in Monty's direction. "*He* figured out that I figured it out."

"Well?" Stark said, turning to Monty. Peaches gave off a low rumble as he padded next to me. "How did he…Is that a hellhound?"

Stark focused completely on Peaches, crouching low to bring his face level with my hellhound. For a moment, I feared Peaches would simply chomp on Stark's head, but all he did was stare back at the strange man.

"How?" Stark said, looking up at me. "How did you manage to capture one alive?"

"Capture?" I said, slightly angry. "I didn't capture him. He's my bondmate. His name is Peaches."

Stark stood and laughed for a good ten seconds before looking at us and realizing I was serious.

"You're serious?" he said, wiping a tear from his eye. "You're bonded to this hellhound? Peaches? You named a hellhound, one of the most devastating creatures on this or any plane, Peaches?"

"I didn't name him. He was a gift," I said, disliking his tone. "The name came with the hellhound."

"A gift?" Stark said, curious now and looking at Peaches again. "*Who* gifted him to you?"

"Hades."

"Hades? *The* Hades?" Stark said, incredulous. "Who *exactly* are you?"

"No one of consequence," I said. "No one you would know, trust me."

"No, seriously, who are you? I must know why, *how* you were gifted a hellhound."

"Get used to disappointment," I said. "Besides, that's not why we're here. Monty?"

"Please excuse my overly-cryptic associate," Monty said. "We've come here to procure an item. My name is Tristan Montague."

"Montague? Montague...I've heard that name before," he said, raising a finger and looking away. "Give me a second; it'll come back to me. Now, where did I hear that name?"

I gave Monty a look. Stark was definitely not playing with a full deck.

"The name is well-known in certain mage circles," Monty began. "Perhaps you've heard it in passing? My uncle Dexter is quite known in disreputable places, like this one."

"Dexter...Dexter Montague," Stark said, snapping his fingers. "Oh, Tessa hates him, and your family. This is starting to make sense. She said he overstepped the bounds, threatened her. She really doesn't like him." He focused on Monty. "Guess she doesn't like you, either, if she sent you here."

"What does that mean?" I said concerned. "What is up with this place?"

"*You* are not a mage," Stark said, turning to me and shaking his head. "Why would she send you? This is a place for mages. What did you do?"

"I guess I'm just special," I said, looking around. "What do you mean, a place for mages?"

"Tessa abrogated the rules set forth by the Golden Circle when she was transferred to the Moving Market," Monty said, matter-of-factly. "I'm surprised my uncle didn't erase her."

"Now you, *you* sound like a mage," Stark said, narrowing his eyes at Monty. "No one says 'abrogate' when they could just say broke the rules...except a mage. Golden Circle, even. I'm impressed. The answer is no, I can't, and besides, you can't afford me."

"I beg your pardon?" Monty said, momentarily flustered. "You haven't even heard my request."

"How much is it?" I said. "Maybe we can afford it."

"Doesn't matter," Stark said. "Did Tessa tell you she'd cover the cost if you made it here alive?"

"Well, yes," Monty admitted. "She said you'd be amenable to providing my request."

Stark laughed again, but this time there was no humor in the sound. He sounded bitter and angry.

"Amenable? Amenable!" Stark yelled while pounding one of the tables. "That bitch."

"I agree with you there," I said. "I'm guessing she lied."

"Your powers of observation are mind-blowing, Mr...?"

"Strong, Simon Strong."

"Right, listen here, Einstein," Stark continued. "I can't create anything for you imbued with power. I mean, with my ability and some raw material I could create a tether for each of you in under five minutes."

"They're that easy to create?"

"No, I'm just that good," Stark said. "But in here"—he motioned with a hand around the space—"not happening. You want to know the cost?"

"It helps to know what we're dealing with, yes."

"Freedom is the cost. I can't create while I'm in here."

"What's all this, then?" I said, pointing to the several projects on the tables. "Decoration?"

"May as well be," Stark said. "It's what I do to keep from going mad. Keeps my mind occupied."

I was about to comment on how unsuccessful that plan had been when Monty gave me a short cough and a subtle head shake, warning me it was a bad idea.

"Are you saying you don't have access to your abilities?"

"That's what I just said," Stark replied, throwing a hand up with a look of annoyance. "Ugh...mages. Ten words when one can do. This part of the seventh ring has been configured to prevent that. Tessa has trapped me here and cut off access to my abilities. There's no way out. That was the whole point of the riddle, to keep others from being trapped in here with me, but you two were *so* clever. You just had to figure it out. Well, welcome to my cell."

"How?" Monty said. "I was able to cast outside."

"I know," Stark said. "Try casting in here."

Monty gestured and whispered something under his breath as Stark placed his weapon on a nearby table, sat on a stool, and watched. Symbols glowed in the air, hung there for about five seconds, and then slowly faded out with a loud *pop*.

"I'm impressed," Stark said. "A whole five seconds. Not bad. The most I could ever manage is three. You clearly possess power, but five seconds' worth won't be enough, sorry."

"Bloody hell," Monty said. "I didn't see it. We walked right into it."

"I'm surprised those things out there didn't shred you," Stark said. "They got here not too long ago, emptied the streets in days. Disgusting aberrations."

"Is he referring to the—"

"Unbound, yes," Monty said. "Did you see if anyone was controlling them?"

"I saw one man who wasn't affected by them," Stark said. "I assumed he was their leader, or master. They swarmed around him, but he seemed unaffected by them. After that, I made sure the door was locked tight."

"That would be Mahnes," Monty said. "This must be his endgame. He convinces us to come to the Market and Tessa provides a location to dispatch us."

"They're working together?"

"It would appear that whatever my uncle said to her left an impression."

"Enough of an impression that she wants you dead?"

"My uncle can be quite menacing," Monty said. "I'm sure he didn't hold back. Besides, he removed her guard dragon. I'm certain she wasn't pleased about that."

"We're screwed, aren't we?"

"You were screwed the moment you stepped into the seventh ring," Stark said. "You just didn't know it yet."

I looked away and cursed under my breath.

TWENTY-FOUR

"Dawning on you, now, is it?" Stark said, looking at Monty. "This place is the ultimate null zone. Tessa inscribed runes everywhere. As an added feature, she added a temporal displacement—damn Time Weaver. Even if I could figure out where the precise lock was, and I have an excellent idea of where the main component lies, we keep shifting around. I'd never keep it in place long enough to open it. My ability is useless in this place."

"What are you talking about?" I said, confused. "You lost your magic?"

Stark stared at me for a few seconds.

"Are you sure Hades gifted a hellhound *to* you?" Stark said. "Maybe he meant to feed *you* to it instead, and it took pity *on* you, not wanting to eat such a dull creature. How have you managed to survive this long?"

"Oh, the shop teacher has jokes," I said. "At least I'm not the one stuck here."

"Wow," Stark said, shaking his head. "Maybe she sent

you here for your own safety? Your dizzying intellect is obviously too powerful for the outside world."

"Finally someone who can appreciate greatness when he sees it," I said. "It's not easy being this awesome. I make genius look easy."

Stark nodded sagely and smiled.

"Tell me, *genius*, how exactly were *you* planning on leaving? You brought an exit with you? Do you think Tessa ever planned on letting the two of you leave? She played you. Just like she played me."

"Shit," I said, properly embarrassed as I realized we were just as stuck as Stark. Tessa pointed the way and we blindly followed the path into the trap. Total amateur hour move. "We're trapped too."

Stark nodded.

"I'll take obvious statements for 100, Art," he said. "Tessa outplayed, outmaneuvered, and outclassed you, genius. No one will ever find you in here. They won't even know you're gone."

"The temporal displacement," Monty said. "It's a loop."

"From what I've been able to figure out, yes. As far as anyone outside the Market knows, you've only been gone a few minutes. Mind you, this is just my theory, but it fits her M.O."

"What did you do?" Monty said, his voice serious. "Why did she trap you in here?"

"It's what I didn't do," Stark said. "She wanted me to create an item. A weapon that would be the second-to-last thing I ever made."

"Second to last? " I said. "Why second to last?"

"Because once the item was complete, the next thing I would be making was something to neutralize it," Stark said. "We disagreed on her having that much power, so she decided to retire me to the seventh ring."

"Why hasn't she had someone else make this item?" Monty said. "Another artificer?"

"Because no one else can," Stark said. "That's why I'm stuck here. She wants me to breakdown and make the confounded thing. Not while I'm breathing!"

"That's why she hasn't eliminated you," Monty said. "She's trying to wear you down until you comply to build it."

"The moment I do, I'm dead one second after I demonstrate how it works."

"What is this thing?" I said. "What did she want you to create?"

"You know what kind of mage she is," Stark said with a sigh. "Do you know what her discipline is?"

"She's a Time Weaver?" I said. "Moves the Moving Market around?"

"With a very specific condition," Stark added. "She needs a locus, some kind of focus, not like a wizard. She needs a locus to exert her full power. Without one, she's diminished, not even at one-third her power."

"She needs to be tethered to a fixed place in space and time in order to exert her full ability?" Monty said. "That is why she was sent to the Moving Market."

"Exactly," Stark said. "Now, imagine all that power untethered. Able to travel wherever and whenever she wanted, no one could stop her. I wasn't going to unleash that on this or any world."

"She wanted to be untethered," I said, putting it together. "That sounds like a bad idea."

"Unimaginably bad," Stark agreed. "If you haven't guessed by now, Tessa isn't exactly a nice person."

"Could you do it?" Monty said. "Create an item to untether her?"

"If I had access to my ability, yes. It would take some time, but I could create something that would allow her to move freely with full use of her power."

"Why did you say no?" I said. "I mean, I'm sure she would've paid you."

"Did you miss the part where I mentioned she's unstable?" Stark said, staring at me. "Besides, I'm an *Anvil and Hammer* Master Artificer."

He said it as if that was self-explanatory. It wasn't.

"Which means what? You only work in a forge with metal?"

"It's the highest level a mage of his ability can attain," Monty said. "The elite level of his craft. Bestowed on one mage every few centuries or so...by dwarves, no less."

"My Order prevents me from making what she wants, violently. You ever seen an angry dwarf? Not a pretty sight, trust me, especially when they bury a hammer in your forehead," Stark said, crossing his arms. "Which means I can't create something that would endanger the world, when corrupted by some insane Time Weaver."

"Psychobatshit mage on a major power trip is more like it," I said. "How long has she kept you here?"

"Not too long," Stark said. "By my reckoning, it's been about ten years."

"How could you even tell?" I said. "This place is locked in time."

"The time loop collapses when I get new supplies," Stark said. "She can't let me die and she can't trap her own people in here. I get food and supplies about once a month. When that happens, the loop softens a bit and I can gauge the flow of time. It's not precise, but I can estimate it. Is it still 1976?"

I turned to look at Monty, who slowly shook his head.

"1976?" Monty said. "Was that the year she trapped you?"

"That's what I reckon the year is," Stark said. "She trapped me in here ten years ago—1966."

"Stark," Monty began, "1966 was fifty-five years ago. It's currently 2021."

Stark's face fell.

"Fifty-Five years?" Stark said, stunned. "Are you certain? She's had me in here for over half a century?"

I nodded.

"I'm sorry," I said. "If it's any consolation, you don't look a day over forty."

"It's not, but thanks," Stark said, dumbfounded. "Fifty-five years? That bitch. I'm...going to need a moment. Excuse me."

Stark left the room.

"Stating the obvious for 100, Art," I said, realizing the reference. "Makes perfect sense—*Jeopardy*."

Monty gave me a quizzical look.

"Yes, we are in jeopardy. Have you not been paying attention?" Monty said, still looking at me oddly. "We have to figure out a way to break or bypass the lock Tessa cast on this place. Are you feeling ill?"

"No, *Jeopardy* is an old TV show...nevermind," I said. "We're screwed, aren't we? I mean he didn't even know he was in here for fifty-five years. How could he not know?"

"You recall when you entered this place? You said it lacked—what did you call it—*umph*?"

"Yes, it feels empty, like something is missing. Like this place is stuck. Even the air feels stale."

"That 'something' you're not feeling is the flow of time, along with a pronounced energy signature," Monty said. "I didn't sense that upon arriving here."

"Then you wouldn't know if time was flowing or not?"

"Exactly," Monty said. "This is a temporal trap for mages. This is why Stark hasn't been able to accurately gauge the passage of time. There's no way he could. He's a mage."

"Well, that explains being off by forty-five years," I said. "It doesn't solve our immediate situation, though. We still have Mahnes and his Unbound to deal with and we need the ethereal tether."

"It's etheric, and our more immediate concern is leaving this place," Monty said, looking around the room. "Once we exit, we can have Stark fashion us the tether."

"Right, but you said it's a mage trap. How are you going to find a way out?"

"True," Monty said. "If only we had *someone* who had access to energy, but wasn't a mage. Do you know of anyone who fits that description?"

"Master Yat?" I volunteered. "He has plenty of access to energy with that staff of his, but he isn't a mage; at least, I've never seen him do any finger wiggles or whisper strange words under his breath, like you do."

"Anyone else besides Master Yat? Someone closer in proximity to our current location would be helpful."

"Not seeing it, sorry," I said, giving it some thought and shaking my head. "Like you said, we're trapped."

Monty stared at me for a good five seconds.

"I really do worry about you sometimes, Simon," he said with a sigh. "It's you."

"Me, what?"

"When Tessa created this trap, she designed it with mages in mind," Monty explained. "She didn't count on an outlier hybrid, someone who could manipulate energy without being a mage."

"That...would be me, sure," I said. "But what exactly is my magic missile going to do in this place? I could punch holes in the walls. Doesn't exactly solve the whole 'being trapped' part of the equation."

"We don't need your magic missile, at least not yet." Monty began his words hesitantly as he thought the process through. "First, you'd have to use your mark. The one that stops time—not the one that has made you lethally popular as of late."

"You want me to stop time inside of a time loop?" I said, confused. "Is that even possible? Won't that break something? Time isn't flowing."

"Not for mages. That's the design of the trap, but for you, even if you don't overtly feel it, time *is* flowing. Perhaps slower than usual, but it *is* flowing."

"And you want me to disrupt that somehow by using my mark?"

"That is the dicey part," Monty said. "The theory is sound, but..."

"Stop," I said, raising a hand. "Every time you start with, 'The theory is sound, but' something either explodes, implodes, or—"

"You're exaggerating," Monty interrupted, waving my

words away. "You've never been imploded. I'm certain I would have noticed."

"Or tries to disintegrate me," I continued. "In the 'reducing me to my component atoms' sort of way. Not the 'cutting me off from my source of power' way. You know, the most painful outcome kind of way."

"You haven't even heard the theory."

"Skip to the side effects if it goes wrong," I said. "What happens if your theory is off—hypothetically, of course—and something goes wrong?"

"The odds of that happening are—" Monty began.

"Astronomically slim," I finished. "I know. Humor me. What happens?"

"You would cause a fracture in the space-time continuum," Monty said, "fragmenting our current timeline and potentially trapping us in an infinite loop of ever-evolving versions of our current situation."

"So, in English, we'd be trapped in here, forever?"

"More or less, yes."

"And if it works?" I said. "What happens if this plan of yours works?"

"Well, theoretically, of course"—Monty rubbed his chin—"it should place us in Carl Schurz Park prior to entering the Moving Market, give or take a few minutes."

"With full knowledge of what happened and meeting Stark?"

"If you're getting out, I'm going with you," Stark said, coming into the room, looking at me. "Is it true you can manipulate energy and stop time?"

"Manipulate? Not so much. I can fire a magic missile."

"A what?" Stark said, looking at Monty. "Magic missile?"

"A concentrated beam of energy he can direct."

"Ah, got it. And this mark of yours that stops time? Show me."

I glanced at Monty who nodded.

"This," I said, showing Stark my hand. "I press this and it stops time for me. Usually for about ten seconds, if everything goes well"—I rubbed my jaw absently—" although it feels much longer sometimes."

"A *Shrivatsa*," Stark said under his breath in awe. "How did you get this? This mark is imbued with more power than I can imagine. Even my teacher couldn't...Who, *what* are you?"

"Complicated," I said. "This was given to me by Kali. Well, she cursed me with it actually."

"First Hades gifts you a hellhound, and then Kali curses you?" Stark said shaking his head. "You either have the most powerful friends or the most dangerous enemies."

"Most days, it's a bit of both."

"May I?" Stark said as he made to touch my mark. "Can I examine it?"

"Sure. Not much to examine," I said, extending my hand in his direction. "It's the world's most dangerous tattoo, imbued with power."

"This is a symbol of extreme power," Stark said, running a finger over my hand and tracing the symbol. "No one in the Order would even attempt this mark...no one. You said Kali *marked* you with this?"

"Yes. She was pissed at the time," I said. "Monty and I interrupted one of her plans. Amazingly, she only chose to curse me."

"I'm surprised she didn't reduce you to dust on the

spot," Stark said before letting go of my hand. "She's not exactly known for her benevolence."

"Tell me about it."

Stark turned to Monty.

"You think he can do it?" Stark said. "He'll have about five to ten seconds on the outside. Your abilities won't return immediately. If he fails, it all goes south and who knows what or when the outcome will be."

"I think he can do it," Monty said. "Do you know where the main lock is?"

"I do," Stark said. "I found it not too long ago. Tessa hid it well, but she's thinking like a mage. I saw it as an engineering problem. Still, she is devious and cruel."

"An engineering problem—of course, that makes sense," Monty said. "Where did she place it?"

Stark pointed to his books.

"She interlaced it into the books," Stark said with venom. "The one thing she knew I would never destroy. Each of those books makes up a component of the null zone and temporal stasis keeping us trapped."

"These books are priceless," Monty said, almost whispering. "Simon would need to destroy at least—"

"Destroy them all," Stark said, his voice hard. "Because of those books, I've lost half a century of my life. Besides, all those books are in here." He tapped the side of his head. "I've memorized them all."

I looked at the bookcase. There were easily one hundred books on it, if not more.

"You memorized all those books?"

"Yes. I have a perfect photographic memory," Stark said. "If you blast them all, I'd still be able to reproduce them. Not that I need to."

"Why didn't you try to destroy them once you found out where the lock was?" I said. "Then you'd be free."

"Free to go where?" Stark said. "I'm an artificer, not a battle mage. I don't teleport. I can create an item that would open a portal, but I would need points of reference I don't have. Teleportation is a complicated and tricky business. I'd rather not end my life in a half-baked escape attempt."

"At least you could've destroyed them, had access to your power?"

"You don't think I tried?"

"I didn't mean to imply—"

"As soon as I discovered the lock, it was my only goal," Stark said, gazing at the books. "Everyday, every waking moment, I would try to find ways to destroy them. Each and every method I used failed."

"Couldn't you have just burned them?"

"Not that simple," Stark said. "This is a loop. If I destroyed them while in the loop, they would simply revert back to their original state. There's also the small matter of my not having access to any real power. Regular fire isn't going to do it; I'd need imbued flame to burn these books."

"Imbued flame?" I said, thinking back to my magic missile. "Not really sure that's what I do."

"Only one way to find out," Stark said, then turned to Monty. "Let me hear the plan."

"Simon will need to cause a pocket of suspended time within the loop," Monty said. "This should cause a polarity shift, reestablishing the flow of time here. He then proceeds to destroy the lock—"

"Reverting the flow to normal once the pocket is

disengaged," Stark finished. "This will give you access to your ability and shunt you back to the moment before you entered the Market, provided he gets the sequence correct."

"Yes. Theoretically, it should work."

"The theory is sound," Stark said, glancing at me. "Do you think he's up to the task?"

Monty nodded. "Can you show him the sequence?"

"So, what exactly am I doing, now?" I asked, concerned. "Can you explain it in non-mage English?"

Stark stepped over to the bookcase and pointed.

"You blast here first"—he moved his hand downward —"here second"—he moved his hand again—"then here. In that order, understand?"

"What happens if I mess up the order?"

"Could be any number of things, none of them pleasant."

"Don't mess up the order, got it."

"Don't mess up the order," Stark repeated, removing one book from the bookcase. It was Ziller's *Permutations*. "This one is safe. Not even Tessa's cast could affect this book."

"How long do we have before Tessa sends someone to check on you once the lock is disrupted?" Monty said. "I would assume the temporal disruption will alert her immediately?"

"The one time I managed to mildly disrupt the lock, she was here within five minutes," Stark said. "I had no access to my abilities in that time. I would imagine the disturbance takes some time to travel to her."

"Once I destroy the books, Tessa will sense a disturbance?"

"I just said that," Stark said, annoyed. "Are you deaf?"

"No, just making it clear, that my actions will cause a disturbance in the energy around the books...a disturbance in the Force."

"Disturbance in the Force?" Stark said, turning to Monty. "What is he going on about?"

"Sometimes it's best to ignore him," Monty said. "Do you have any transient chalk? Green, if possible."

"Actually, I do. Didn't work for me, didn't have enough time, but I'm guessing it will work for you."

Stark went to one of the tables and rummaged around in the drawer. After a few seconds, he came back with a large piece of green chalk and handed it to Monty.

"This will do," Monty said, looking at the chalk. "What potency level is it?"

"Five, I think," Stark said. "As long as she hasn't moved the Market to Europe, we should be fine."

"And if she has?" I said, looking at Monty draw a large circle in the corner of the room. "What happens if she's moved the Market?"

"I'm guessing you came in from North America, right?"

"Upper East Side, yes."

"Level-five chalk should be fine, *if* we're in the same country," Stark said. "It's not powerful enough to teleport us across an ocean. He won't have access to his power for some time after the null zone is disrupted. That circle should help speed things along."

"Can't you just create your own circle?" I said, looking at Monty. "This sounds dangerous."

"I could, but I'd rather not face Tessa or the Doorman defenseless while we are still in a null zone. This circle will act as a power booster to my own abilities. We'll be fine."

"I'm not an expert on anything having to do with teleportation, but how do we take Stark with us once we leave?" I said. "I get that your intransigent circle will amplify the teleportation, but won't that be negated by the fact that Tessa created this trap for him?"

"Not bad," Stark said, looking at me approvingly. "Even a broken clock is right twice a day." Stark turned to Monty. "You'll have to compensate for any specific parts of the temporal loop keyed to my signature and amplify your output of power accordingly."

"*That* would be dangerous," Monty said with a frown. "I could inadvertently bring more than the three of us."

"What about the hellhound?" Stark said. "You can't abandon him here."

"I will do no such thing," Monty said, looking at Peaches. "He has an errand to run."

"A what?" I said, surprised. "What do you mean he has an errand? He's not a delivery hellhound."

"He's not making a delivery, he's picking someone up."

"You want to send a hellhound to pick someone up? What is he going to do after he gives this person a heart attack?"

"Not to worry—the intended person is scarier than your hellhound."

"You're not being specific enough," I said. "Do you realize how many people we know who fit that description?"

Monty finished drawing the circle and stepped over to Peaches, crouching down in front of him. He placed a hand on my hellhound's massive head and looked into his eyes.

"This brave hellhound is going to find my uncle and

bring him to us," Monty said, looking straight at Peaches. "Can you do that once we restore the flow of time?"

<Tell the angry man I can find the old bird man, if he promises to make me three sausages, big ones.>

<Three sausages? Really?>

<I would ask for more, but I'm saving that for an emergency.>

"It's going to cost you three sausages," I said. "He's actually giving you a discount. I'd take it if I were you."

"Wait," Stark said, interrupting. "You can speak to it?"

"Him, not it, and yes, I can," I said, annoyed. "Like I said...I'm complicated. Deal, Monty?"

"If he's successful, five sausages"—Monty held up a hand with the fingers splayed—"extra large. Agreed?"

Peaches chuffed and vibrated in place with a low rumble.

"Astounding," Stark said, cocking his head to one side. "It—I mean, he understands you."

"I'll take that as a yes," Monty said, getting to his feet. "Now it's just a matter of disabling the lock. Ready, Simon?"

"I've never felt less ready for anything in my life," I said. "Are you sure my magic missile is going to work?"

"Has it ever failed you in the past?"

"You mean after it transformed from the anemic missile?"

"Yes, afterwards," Monty said, placing a hand on my shoulder. "I seem to recall a mound of slag that was once a trailer after we dealt with Douglas. Ramirez never did discover what happened to that trailer."

"I can neither confirm nor deny the existence of said trailer."

Monty nodded with a small smile.

"Your missile will be fine. Just remember the sequence."

"I'm ready."

TWENTY-FIVE

Monty and Stark moved over to the circle.

Before he stepped inside, Stark grabbed a few metal rings from one of the tables, and stuffed them in his pockets.

"You want tethers?" Stark said when Monty raised an eyebrow at him. "I can't make them out of thin air, you know. These will work in the short term—probably one use only, but they'll work."

Stark stepped in the circle, clutched Ziller's *Permutations* to his chest and nodded.

"Whenever you're ready, Simon," Monty said, brushing off the chalk dust from his hand. "Remember the sequence."

I patted Peaches on the head and motioned for him to go stand next to Monty and Stark. If something went wrong, I figured it would happen near me. I didn't want him caught in any kind of backlash or time beam slamming my location.

Peaches padded silently over to Monty and rumbled.

I reached over and pressed my hand on my mark. For a few seconds, the endless knot, given to me courtesy of Kali, gave off a golden light which increased in intensity until I had to look away.

"Nothing like a supernova on your hand to blind you," I muttered, looking away as everything slowly grew out of focus. "One day, I'm going to figure out what these colors mean."

The heady smell of lotus blossoms and earth after a hard rain filled my lungs. This was followed by the sharp smell of cut oranges and an aroma hinting of cinnamon permeating the air.

"No, no, no, not now," I whispered, shaking my head before looking around. "Not this time."

The sensation of time coming to an abrupt standstill was profound. The flecks of chalk dust still lingered, frozen in the air near Monty. This sensation was unlike the other times. This time, time stopped cold.

"Splinter, you're still alive," Karma said, looking around. "We really have to stop meeting like this."

She was dressed in a burnt-sienna sundress which flowed around her as if she had her own personal breeze. Her hair was loose and hung around her shoulders and neck. She wore a silver chain which held a large, ruby red B. She was barefoot and padded silently over to one of the stools nearest me.

"Hello, Karma," I said, taking in the outfit. "This is a new look. Heading to the shore? A little vacation?"

She looked down at her dress.

"I don't do vacations, ever. Occasionally, it may appear I'm lax in my duties, but I catch up to everyone...sooner or later. Now, this situation looks fun."

"You and I have different definitions of fun."

"I know. You really need to get out more. So much to see and do," she said. "There are entire planes you haven't visited and destroyed."

"For the record—"

"Shhh," she said, putting a finger to her lips and cupping a hand around her ear. "Do you hear that?"

"No, what?"

"That's the sound of me not caring about your pity party," she said with a smile. "Why don't you own it?"

"Own what?"

"The destruction," she said. "If I were you, I"d make it part of my name: Simon, Destroyer of Cities, Crusher of Hopes, Drinker of the Dark Death Brew."

"Seems a little long, don't you think?"

"True, but it is catchy, and considering your recent upgrade"—she tapped her forehead—"you will be facing some nasty new friends. Nice work on the ogre by the way."

"Thanks," I said. "Any clue on what I'm doing here?"

Karma glanced over at the bookcase then at the frozen Monty, Stark, and Peaches.

"Hmm, let's see... You seem to be trapped in a temporal loop and are using your limited but potent ability to step out of the flow of time to destroy the lock, hoping it restores the flow in this place and allows you to escape, yes?"

"Pretty much. Any pointers?"

"Splinter," she said, wagging a finger. "You know I can't help you."

"Not asking for help just some pointers. You know, karmic advice?"

She stared at me for a few seconds before smiling again. Her smile did nothing to put me at ease.

"You are fortunate I am interested in seeing the outcome of your actions," she said finally. "You do make my life interesting, even if it means extra paperwork. What do you want to know?"

I let out a low sigh and kept my distance, hoping to keep my face slap-free.

"Will it work?"

"Will what work? Specifics, Splinter, use your words."

"If I destroy the books in the sequence they suggested, will it work?"

"Is that what the mage brain trust said?"

I nodded.

"You're taking advice from a mildly-addled mage who has been trapped for half a century, and another who is recovering from a schism that altered his mind?"

"*Well*, when you put it *that* way," I said, realizing the danger. "So it won't work?"

"Ever since you set foot in the Market, you've been following a path set for you," Karma said. "What makes you think this is any different?"

"I don't understand."

"The forces arrayed against you know how mages think. Hasn't it been obvious? The message, the Market, and now this. The only thing they can't anticipate is you."

"If I act like a mage, then we fall further into the trap."

"They've tried to factor for you and your behavior by neutralizing any impact you may have. This is why you find yourself in a null zone."

"The null zone was for me?"

"Not just for you," she said. "It's meant to act as a buffer against you."

"I still don't understand."

"I know," she said with a nod. "Understanding is not something I can give you. No one can give you that."

"Do you know what happens if I destroy the lock in the sequence they suggested?"

Her face darkened for a brief moment.

"You're skirting the edge there," she said. "All I can say is that it won't work. You may want to consider a new sequence."

"A new sequence? Are you kidding me? I don't have time to consider a new sequence."

"Actually, right now, while I'm here, you have plenty of time. Think, 'How did you end up in here?' and do the same thing. That's as much as I can say, and it's going to give me hours of corrective action and paperwork."

"That makes absolutely no sense," I said, exasperated. "We had to answer a riddle to even get in here."

"Exactly," she said, standing as I panicked. It meant she was going to leave soon, and I still had no clue as to what she meant. "One more thing, seeing as I'll have to do a mountain of paperwork anyway: whether you figure out the correct sequence or not, prepare for someone to die."

Her dress flowed in her personal breeze as she looked at Monty and Stark. She glided over to where I stood.

"What are you talking about?"

"I thought I was being clear," she said, turning to me. "You have a choice. You can figure out the correct sequence—which will allow you to step out of this place into a direct conflict, think kettle and fire—or, you could do nothing. Either way, someone dies."

She stepped close and ran a fingernail along my jaw.

"I can't be responsible for them, for anyone, dying."

"Some are born great, some achieve greatness, and some have greatness thrust upon them," she said, tapping me on the cheek and jarring my brain. "Think of this situation as one enormous thrust into your greatness."

"This is wrong," I said when I could think straight again. "Either way I'm fu—"

"Shhh," she said, putting a finger on my lips. "No one cares, Splinter. Time for you to make a choice. I look forward to seeing which one it is. Once I leave, you have ten seconds. Don't waste them."

She disappeared a moment later.

My mind raced to how we entered Stark's shop. I deciphered the riddle, Monty asked me the question, and then he input the answer. What were his exact words? How did he put the answer? *I just implemented the inverse order application.*

"Inverse order," I muttered to myself as I extended an arm at the bookcase and took a deep breath. "The sequence has to be inverted."

TWENTY-SIX

I focused and thought back to Master Yat's words: "*You must find the way around the obstacles. Find a way to circumvent null zones. If you can step out of the flow of time, you can step into the flow of energy.*"

Step into the flow.

I took a deep breath and let my senses expand. The little voice in the back of my head was telling me I only had a few seconds left. I muzzled it and locked it in a closet as it protested my abuse.

There was energy flowing around me. Even with my eyes closed, I could sense the runes everywhere. All I had to do was stop looking for them to see them clearly.

Now *I* was sounding like Yat.

A path of energy became apparent as I opened my eyes.

"*Ignisvitae*," I whispered, feeling the draw of power from my body as energy coalesced around my hand.

A beam of violet energy exploded from my hand.

I concentrated on keeping it focused and destroyed the

lock in opposite from the order Stark had given me, hoping I was doing the right thing and not making things worse.

The beam engulfed the books, turning them to dust. I managed to destroy the last set of books as time snapped back into place.

"What did you do?" Stark said as I stepped over to the circle. "The sequence..." He looked at the bookcase, then at Monty. "He did it wrong. You've killed us."

"No," I said, my voice firm. "You were wrong. You both were. The order of the sequence had to be inverted. Like the answer to the riddle."

Stark opened his mouth to speak and then closed it.

"He's right," Monty said. "I can't believe I didn't see that. How did you know?"

"I didn't," I said. "Karma gave me some major clues."

"Karma?" Stark said. "What kind of answer is *that*? You're not a mage. How did you know?"

"We don't have the time to get into details right now," Monty said. "Tessa—or more likely the Doorman—is coming here now. We need to leave."

"This whole time, Mahnes and Tessa have been anticipating our moves," I said. "They're playing chess and we're playing checkers. We need to switch it up on them. Before you start that circle, where's the last place you would go? You have to stop thinking like you do, and think non-magey."

"Non-magey?" Monty said as he placed his hands on the symbols in the circle. "We can't go far with this chalk, but I know one place."

"Good," I said, my voice filled with urgency. "Take us there."

Monty pressed more of the symbols and began gesturing. The circle pulsed with energy and the green chalk began to glow, getting brighter with each second.

The symbols flashed, blinding me for a few seconds, and the shop was gone.

When my vision cleared, we were standing in the middle of a small green lawn surrounded by high brick walls. We had arrived in the city near nightfall—at least I hoped it was my city.

The space we stood in was about one fourth the size of a city block. It was serene and somehow removed from the noise and frenetic activity of the city. It was a small oasis of peace nestled in the center of an otherwise chaotic environment.

There were two rows of small wooden benches evenly spaced in the center of the grass. In front of each bench grew a small tree with flowers, partially obscuring the view of the wall behind it.

On the wall, I could make out what seemed to be plaques with names, stacked three high and running along the length of the wall on both sides of the lawn. All around us were the rear of buildings making the lawn seem out of place in the middle of all that brick and concrete.

All around us I could see the softly glowing violet symbols on the walls.

"What is this place?" I said, looking around. "This is either the tiniest cemetery ever or the creepiest park I've been in. Why is it runed?"

"It's the New York Marble Cemetery," Monty said, walking over to one of the older-looking plaques. The name on the plaque read Montague. "Below us are underground vaults. I had my uncle place Connor, my father, here. The runes are a protective measure."

"Your dad is here?"

Monty nodded and turned as Stark moved to one of the benches and sat down. He pulled out the metal rings and started working on them, muttering under his breath.

"What's wrong with him?" I said. "What's he doing?"

"No time...no time... This will have to do," Stark kept mumbling. "I kept my end. I held up my end."

"Monty," I said warily. "That doesn't sound good. Is he losing it completely?"

"Ask your creature to find my uncle, *now*," Monty said, his voice laced with concern. "I have a feeling we may need his assistance."

<Hey, boy? Can you find the old bird man? Monty's uncle?>

<I can, but can the angry man make some meat now? I'm so hungry and Frank says it's never good to work on an empty stomach.>

<Let me ask. Then you have to go fast, and for the record, your stomach is hardly ever empty.>

"Could you make him some meat for the road?" I said. "I'm sure it will speed up the process."

Monty gestured and formed a large sausage that was immediately evaporated from sight by my hellhound.

<Don't forget your manners. Say thank you.>

<That was so good. I can find the old bird man now.>

Peaches chuffed and gave Monty a low rumble before blinking out.

"Where exactly are we?" I said, looking at the buildings that encircled us. "Is this downtown?"

"41 1/2 2nd Avenue and 2nd Street to be precise," Monty said, focusing on Stark. "Something is wrong."

My phone rang. I connected the call, putting it on speakerphone.

"Strong!" Jarman's voice came through on the line. Behind her I could hear yelling, screams, and gunfire. "Where the hell have you been?"

"What are you talking about?" I said, confused at the interrogation. "We just spoke yesterday."

"Yesterday? Are you insane? That was two days ago. I've been trying to reach you all day! Where have you been?"

"Two days?" I stared at Monty, who returned my look of confusion. "We haven't been gone more than a few hours, right? Are you sure it's been two days?"

"Look," Jarman said, "I don't know what kind of medication you're on, but you need to snap out of it and rendezvous on my location. We've had three more attacks since you disappeared, and there's a swarm of those zombies headed downtown. They just suddenly mobilized. Where are you?"

"We *are* downtown," I said with a sinking feeling. "How many of these things are we looking at?"

"A few thousand," Jarman said. "Everything below 14th Street is a no-man's land. Find someplace safe to hole up and I'll have someone from my team pick you up after the airstrike."

"Airstrike? What airstrike? What do you mean...airstrike?"

"The brass authorized the use of extreme force," Jarman said. "This situation is getting out of control. If they are concentrating their forces, this may be our only chance to take them all out. You need to get to safety. We're tracking their movement and will deploy once they stop moving. Where are you? I'll send a vehicle to pick you up."

Monty shook his head.

"The last thing you want your people doing is picking us up," Monty said. "Whatever you do, keep your people above 4th Street. We know where the Unbound are headed."

"How could you possibly know that?" Jarman said. "They move around randomly, attacking in swarms."

"Except that now they seemed to have organized, moving with direction?"

"Yes, they broke off their attacks and moved *en masse*...downtown."

"Mahnes?" I asked, looking at Monty. "It's him."

Monty nodded and then walked over to Stark.

"Kath," I said, "can't explain right now, but keep your people away from the Village—and whatever you do hold that airstrike. I repeat, do *not* order that airstrike. There are people down here."

"I know," Jarman said her voice grim. "If we don't stop them, we lose the whole city."

"That's hundreds of people."

"Against over eight million in the city," Jarman said. "I'm not going to lose the entire city, Strong. My people tell me the blast will be contained."

"Just keep your people out of the Village."

"The Village is a big place, Strong," Jarman said. "Where are you?"

"New York Marble Cemetery, 2nd and 2nd. Anything below 4th and above Houston is a death sentence right now," I said. "Keep your people out of NOHO."

"We'll form a cordon around your immediate area, but

I'm going to be stretched thin," Jarman said. "We've taken heavy casualties. These things are ferocious at night. I can buy you some time, but if we get a chance to wipe them all out, I'm taking it. I hope you know what you're doing."

"Me too," I said, ending the call and walking over to Monty, who was speaking with Stark. "I bought us some time, but I don't think she's going to wait once the Unbound gather. What's going on?"

"Stark was just explaining how he was leading Mahnes to us," Monty said arms crossed. "Isn't that right?"

My hand reflexively reached for Grim Whisper.

"Talk. Make it fast," I said, drawing my weapon. "You have three seconds to convince me not to end you here and now."

"They have my family," Stark said. "Tessa took them. Promised if I cooperated, gave them you two, she would let them go."

"And you believed her?" I said, raising my voice in anger and frustration. "This whole time, you've been playing us?"

"Not me. Tessa and Mahnes," Stark said with a shudder. "They have my wife and little girl. What choice did I have? I had to cooperate. You haven't seen what those Unbound can do."

I thought back to the scene at the NYTF Seward Park Hub.

"I have," I said my voice dark. "How are you doing it? How do they know to come here? How are you leading them here?"

"Runic tracker," Monty said, "in *this*." He took Ziller's *Permutations* from Stark. "The entire book is a beacon."

"Can we destroy it?" I said, looking at the book with disgust. "I could blast it—"

"No, that would set off a detonation," Monty said. "It's what they would expect."

"I'm sorry," Stark said. "I had to. They were going to kill them if I didn't."

I didn't have the heart to tell them that his family was probably gone. I holstered Grim Whisper and looked at Monty, who, judging from the look on his face, was thinking the same thing.

"Can't we just teleport it away or something?" I said. "I mean, they're tracking the book, not us."

"Mahnes would expect that," Monty said, shaking his head. "The beacon has an origination rune component."

"A what?"

"If I teleport it away, it can still disclose the point of origin from where it was teleported," Monty said, looking up into the now night sky. "Besides we don't have enough time. They're too close."

"Here," Stark said, holding out two metal rings to us. They were covered in small glowing runic script. "Take them before it's too late."

"What are these?" I said, eyeing the rings suspiciously. "More deception?"

"Tethers," Stark said. "Etheric tethers. One use only."

"You really think we're going to—"

Monty took the ring, put it on, and gave me a nod.

"They're safe," Monty said. "His motives are questionable, but these runes are real."

I took the other ring, examined it for a few seconds and grudgingly put it on.

"If this is another con," I said, "you will regret it, shop teacher."

"I know you don't have any reason to trust me," he said. "I'm no fool, I know my family is probably gone, but there's a slim chance of hope if you stop Mahnes. I have an artifact..." He looked to either side. "I made an artifact that can save them."

Stark pulled out another ring. This one was silver, laced with red runes along its surface. He looked at it for a few seconds, and then handed it to Monty.

"That's a—" Monty began.

"I know," Stark said. "This can do it."

"I can't," Monty said. "You need to do this."

"If I don't make it," Stark said, pushing the ring into Monty's hand, "promise me you'll save them."

Monty put the ring in a pocket with a nod.

"I promise."

"I'd say this is a perfect site for a last stand," a voice said above us. "We can even save on the burial arrangements, by just scattering what's left of you among the flowers. Fitting, I think."

I looked up to see a figure covered in a swirl of black energy. Around him were the misshapen figures I could only assume were the Unbound. The man was wearing the usual mageiform: black suit, black shirt, blood red tie.

"Mahnes," Monty said, looking up. "Have you come to get your hands dirty?"

"I don't play with filth." He looked at the Unbound around him. "I have them for that. I have to admit, though, that this last move almost caught me by surprise. If it wasn't for my hidden hand, it would have been much harder to find you."

"Let Stark's family go," I said. "Are you that much of a coward you need to kidnap his family? Why did you take them?"

"I'm a pragmatist. I needed him to cooperate, and his family provided the leverage. It was a simple equation."

"Pragmatist my ass. You're a coward using them against Stark."

"Coward?" Mahnes said with venom. "I'm not a coward. I'm a *god*."

"Whoa, delusions of grandeur much?" I said. "You're one confused mage."

"Simon," Monty said under his breath. "I don't think that's Mahnes, at least not entirely."

"What?" I said, glancing at Monty. "What do you mean that's not Mahnes?"

"Look at his energy signature. It may *look* like Mahnes, but that's no longer him."

"Holy shit," I said after looking closer at Mahnes. The cold grip of fear threatened to strangle the words from my throat. "That's...not Mahnes. Chaos?"

Monty nodded.

"Partially, at least," Monty said, keeping his voice low. "It's no wonder Tessa cooperated. He dwarfs her power, even in the Moving Market."

"I'll make sure to kill you last, Marked of Kali," Chaos/Mahnes said with a small laugh. "I want you to see everyone you care for suffer and die first, and then, when despair has filled you and you beg me for mercy, I'll start killing their families. When no one is left, I *will* end you."

I drew Grim Whisper and realized this was possibly the last time I'd do so. Master Yat's words came back to me: "*If I were the one trying to eliminate this threat, I would start with you.*"

"All I'm hearing is plenty of talk and no action," I said. "You want to get to the killing? I'm your huckleberry. Bring it."

"Kill them," Chaos said. "Bring me the marked one alive."

The Unbound screeched into the night and leapt off the roof, running straight for us.

TWENTY-SEVEN

"Are you trying to hasten our deaths?" Monty said, forming two orbs of bright white and casting them upward. The night turned into day as the orbs grew brighter. "This should slow them down."

The Unbound did slow down under the bright light, but it didn't stop their advance.

"Slow them down?" I said, firing Grim Whisper and dropping several of the Unbound. "How do we stop them? I don't want to slow them down. Dying slowly is still dying, you just get to suffer through the process."

"We need as many as he can control down here with us, "Monty said, as he backed up. "Don't let them get too close."

"Are you insane?" Then I glanced over at the cowering artificer as the Unbound closed on our location. "Stark get over here!" I yelled as Stark ran behind us and kept going to the far wall. "All of sudden you want to get friendly with the soul zombies?"

"This, from the person antagonizing a god? Your diplomacy needs some serious polishing."

"Demi-god," I corrected as I kept firing. "He's only a half a god, and mostly a homicidal dark mage."

"Is that supposed to be better?" Monty said, unleashing a barrage of orbs that slammed into the Unbound, launching them back. He gestured and put up a lattice of golden energy that prevented them from getting closer. "Do *not* use your magic missile or your blade."

"What? This would be the perfect time to use my magic missile," I said. "I could blast them all at once."

"Were you not paying attention? We need as many as he can control down here, with us."

"Do we have a ballpark on that number? Because it doesn't seem like he's slowing down or anything," I said backing up. "They keep coming."

"He has a limit. We just haven't reached it."

"Oh, good—glad to know he has a limit. What is it? One, two thousand?"

"Just make sure to only use your gun."

"My gun is amazing, but it doesn't create infinite rounds," I said. "At some point, I'm going to need to fall back on another weapon."

"I'm working on it."

Monty crouched down and began gesturing, placing his hands on the grass.

"Are you praying for the end, Montague?" Chaos called out from the roof with a laugh. "I'll make sure your death is long and painful, mage. It's the least I can do for Strong."

"Fuck you and the horse you rode in on, Chaos," I said, under my breath, firing at the Unbound trying to claw their way around the lattice. "A little speed would be good here, Monty. That lattice isn't going to hold them forever. Did you lose a contact? What are you doing?"

"Activating the defenses," Monty said, without looking up. "If you let me focus I can get this done."

"I'm sorry, I didn't mean to interrupt you. It's just that there's the small matter of Unbound trying to get to us and we're running out of real estate here."

"Stark, did you find it?" Monty called out without looking up. "Should be on the right."

"Found it!" Stark yelled back, fear clear in his voice. "Ready when you are!"

"Found what?" I said, risking a quick glance at Stark's location. "What is he looking for?"

"The entrance to the vaults below us," Monty said. "Be ready to fall back on my signal. Bloody hell, where is my uncle? Are you certain your creature can find him?"

"For five sausages? Peaches could find you a sense of humor. Give him some time and he'll find Dex."

"Time is the one thing in short supply," Monty said looking up. "He's close to his limit Get ready."

I looked ahead at the mass of Unbound behind the lattice. More were crawling over the walls and down the sides of the building around us.

"Okay, that's officially creeping me out," I said, watching the Unbound scale the walls. "They shouldn't be able to do that."

"Surrender," Chaos called from the roof. "You must understand your situation is hopeless."

"Hopeless?" I called out. "Hopeless is our specialty."

"Don't engage him," Monty said. "He's just trying to unnerve you."

"I *am* unnerved, and running out of ammo. Whatever you're going to do, you'd better do it fast. That lattice isn't holding much longer."

"I never expected to use these defenses in this way, but needs must," Monty said, placing a hand in the grass and turning it counterclockwise. "Move back, Simon."

"Don't have to tell me twice," I said, backpedaling to the wall behind us. "Now what?"

"I've modified the defenses to act as a siphon," Monty started. "As long as the Unbound are contained within the walls of the cemetery, they will be drained of energy. It should make quick work of"—Then Monty looked up, and I followed his gaze. "Oh no. Not now. It would seem Jarman ran out of patience. Bloody hell!"

I saw the streaks of flame cross the night sky and arc in our direction.

"What are we looking at here?" I said, tracking the streaks of flame. "Are those conventional rockets?"

"Missiles, to be precise. Several of them, actually," Monty said and gestured. "This would be a good time for your Dawnward. That's runic ordnance heading our way."

"Runic ordnance? What the hell is runic ordnance and why is it headed our way? Why would the NYTF brass authorize the use of runic rockets?"

"The NYTF is equipped with heavy weapons to deal with major threats," Monty said as a large golden shield appeared in front of us. "I figured Ramirez never requested their use in the past because it has one major drawback."

"Oh, really?" I said in disbelief as the missiles turned and headed our way. "Let me guess: once those missiles hit, this place gets turned into a crater?"

"It would appear Director Jarman thoroughly believes in a scorched-earth policy," Monty said, reinforcing the shield with another layer. "This shield won't be enough. Get your dawnward up, or we get to be part of the collateral damage."

"Maybe we should...oh, I don't know, *evacuate ground zero?*"

"There are residents in this neighborhood," Monty said, flexing his jaw. "If we don't contain that blast, Chaos will have even more Unbound serving him."

"He can take the dead...?"

"Soulless? Unbound? What did you think ripping the soul from your body meant? The Unbound are the recently dead."

"I think I hate him even more now," I said, looking up at Chaos. "What the hell is Jarman thinking?"

"She's thinking this is an extreme situation that requires extreme measures," Monty said. "We have about twenty seconds before those missiles hit."

"She's sending them to *our* location? Is she insane?"

"Did you happen to tell her our location?"

"I may have mentioned it in passing, yes," I admitted. "That's no reason to target us."

"It makes sense," Monty said. "We come back from a few days absence and the Unbound suddenly converge downtown. It's not a coincidence; she's taking a calculated risk. I would have done the same in her position."

"So, she's targeting us?"

"She's targeting them," Monty said, pointing to the Unbound. "As far as she's concerned, she's dealing with a threat to the entire city. Remove the tumor to save the body. Sacrifice a few blocks to save an entire city. In her mind, this is an acceptable loss."

"No it isn't, at least not in my mind."

"Agreed. Dawnward? Anytime now would be good."

"Give me a second," I said, holding up a hand. "This isn't as easy as it looks."

"Wouldn't want to rush you," Monty said, looking up. "Take your time. Stark"—Monty motioned for him to step closer—"it's not safe over there. Why don't you stand over here near us?"

"I don't see how it's safer over there," Stark grumbled. "We're trapped in this place. Our best bet is to go underground. At least there we have a fighting chance."

"Not yet," Monty said, glancing at me. "Any second now, Simon is about to provide us with the ultimate defense. Ready when you are, shield-warrior."

I glared at Monty and took a deep breath, feeling the energy within. I closed my eyes, calmed the conflicting emotions swirling inside, and focused on the strongest one —rage.

Rage that Mahnes would attack us, that he let himself be used by Chaos; that Kali marked me and made my life even harder. I raged that we were currently about to be reduced to atoms by this airstrike. I raged at it all, feeling powerless and small.

I felt the energy rush out of me as I opened my eyes. We were under a dome of violet energy. It was larger than I remembered, but I wasn't complaining.

"What is this?" Stark said in awe. "This is—"

"Impressive," Monty finished with a nod as he stepped out of the dome. "Be right back. Can't do this from in here."

"Where are you going? I thought the whole point of this was to keep us safe?"

"It is," Monty said, gesturing. "I just need to do one thing. You may want to brace for impact."

Monty unleashed a barrage of golden runes which encircled the perimeter of the cemetery, then rushed into the Dawnward. The missiles crashed into us a few seconds later, blinding us with violet and orange light.

TWENTY-EIGHT

I lay on my back and looked into the night sky.

The ringing in my ears made it impossible to hear anything else. My body flushed hot as it dealt with the damage. I felt like one large bruise; even blinking hurt. Stark was unconscious next to me, and Monty stood unsteadily by my side.

I got to my feet and nearly fell over again.

"Welcome back," Monty said. "Good to see you made it."

Monty's suit was a shredded mess. Parts of his face were bruised and covered with blood. The lawn of the cemetery resembled a bombed-out warzone. The wall surrounding us appeared to have taken tank shells. Huge holes exposed the street to either side of us.

"Sorry about the suit."

"Occupational hazard, it seems."

"What...what happened?" I said, still groggy. "Where's Chaos?"

Monty pointed ahead of us. Standing across the empty cemetery lawn stood Chaos. He was gesturing, sending black symbols into the night.

"I see...he made it too," I said. "The Unbound? Did she get them all?"

Monty nodded.

"They're gone, for now," Monty said. "More are on the way, and the integrity of the defenses are gone. We won't be able to contain them this time."

"You look like shit," I said, checking my magazines. "I mean that in the best way possible."

"You don't look much better," Monty said. "Chaos, however, is unscathed."

"Of *course* he is. I'm down to two magazines," I said. "You think entropy rounds will do more than tickle him?"

"Let's find out. We can't let him finish that sequence, or things will get bad."

"Really?" I said, drawing Grim Whisper. "You mean it's been good up till now?"

Monty nodded and began gesturing. White orbs formed in his hands as we closed on Chaos.

"We're still alive. I'd say that's good. Use whatever you need to against him. In fact, use everything."

"I guess this is the part where we get to take down the dark mage god."

"Or die trying."

Monty unleashed his orbs as I extended an arm.

"*Ignisvitae!*" I yelled and opened fire with Grim Whisper. "Die, you motherfu—!"

Chaos extended a hand and caused another explosion to rock the cemetery, slamming us against what remained of the back wall. My magic missile and Monty's orbs crashed into Chaos—who batted them away with a backhand as he laughed.

"Is this all you have? Pitiful. You both deserve death."

"Monty?" I said, feeling real fear as I leaned against the wall to catch my breath. "That didn't even scratch him."

"I'm aware, but we have bigger problems."

"Bigger?"

Then I heard the sound. It was the sound of vehicles and boots. The NYTF was moving in.

Chaos turned at the sound and smiled at us.

"It would seem my reinforcements have arrived," Chaos said. "As you said, let's get to the dying, shall we?"

Chaos swung an arm around, and black energy raced outward from his position in a semi-circle. The arc of black energy exploded through what remained of the walls and kept racing outward. Monty threw up a shield and deflected the blast. Moments later, all around us we heard the dying screams of NYTF officers.

I heard Chaos laugh as the men and women of the NYTF died. Many of them collapsed the moment they set foot on the lawn. Others died outside the walls, but I could hear their agony as their lives were ripped from their bodies.

"Who...what the hell is that?" I heard Jarman say from behind me. "Montague, Strong, you need to get out of here now."

I nearly jumped forward when she spoke.

"How did you get back here?" I said, staring at her. "This place is a lethal warzone."

"I was on the outer edge of the cordon," Jarman said.

"You have this place lit up like a stadium. It wasn't that hard to find you—I just followed the sound of destruction."

I looked back and noticed that the wall that had been standing behind us seconds ago was mostly gone. The only portion that remained was as wide as the shield Monty had created to deflect the blast.

"Kath, you need to pull your people out now," I said, getting my bearings. "He's going to kill them all."

"Is he the cause of the—oh my god," Jarman said. "What is he doing?"

Black shapes rose from the bodies of the dead NYTF officers.

"He's creating more Unbound," Monty said, his voice and expression grim. "We need to contain this, now. We need to go underground."

"Underground?" Jarman said. "We can't go into the subway with those things chasing us. It'll be a massacre."

"Underground, as in the vaults below us," I said.

"Where we're going, everyone is dead," Monty said, moving quickly to the right and pulling open a concealed door leading to a staircase heading down. "The Unbound will only track the living."

"Kath, give the order to fall back," I said, grabbing Stark and lifting him to his feet. "We'll lead the Unbound away."

"Everyone, fall back! I repeat, fall back behind the cordon!" Jarman yelled into her shoulder radio. "Do you copy? Anyone? Copy?"

Silence.

"How many people were in this initial strike force?" I

asked as we headed down into the enormous vaults. "How many?"

Jarman gave me a stunned look.

"Two hundred, four groups of fifty," she said in shock. "Are you saying that thing up there killed all my people?"

"And turned them into something worse," Monty said, leading the way with an orb of golden light. "We need to move. The Unbound won't remain up there indefinitely."

Monty gestured, activating a large orange rune on the door.

"You sealed it well," Stark said. "That's one strong barrier."

"It won't hold them for long," Monty said. "We need to find a way to neutralize Mahnes."

"This place is immense," I said, looking around. "Is there another exit besides the one we just used?"

"Yes," Monty said. "We can't use it yet. We have to stop Chaos here."

"How exactly are we going to do that?" I said. "Did you see what he did to my magic missile? He swatted it away."

"Along with my orbs," Monty said. "I'd say facing him is going to be problematic."

"Problematic? More like suicidal. We can't beat Chaos, he's too strong."

"We don't need to beat Chaos, we need to beat Mahnes."

"Who is currently being inhabited by Chaos. Plus, I don't have a negation rune handy—do you? Because I don't see another way of exorcising him."

"He's an old god, not a demon; but, exorcising... That may be it." Monty turned to Stark. "The tethers: can you rework them if I gave you the proper runes?"

"I'd need a new ring. What I gave you is all I had," Stark said. "What were you thinking?"

"Instead of using the tethers as a defense, can they be reworked to be used offensively?"

"I guess it could work," Stark said. "I've never heard of a tether being used as a weapon. They've always been used as protection."

"Simon," Monty said, extending a hand, "your ring."

"We're entering the experimental-magic area again, aren't we?" I said handing him my tether. "Because this sounds like flying by the seat of your pants—only, we aren't wearing pants and we aren't flying. It's more like falling at speed off a very high cliff, building wings *on the way down*, with Chaos waiting for us at the bottom."

"I understand your reticence, and if you have any suggestions, I'm open to ideas," Monty said, taking the ring. "We can stop here, this will do."

We entered a large courtyard area and Monty circled around the central space, pacing methodically around its circumference.

Monty kept moving as he placed the rings in his hands, cupping them both around them. He whispered something under his breath and his hands took on a deep blue glow. He stood still and then said something else I couldn't quite make out.

When he opened his hands, there was only one bluish-black ring in his palm.

"Don't we need two of those?" I said, looking at the ring. "You know to protect *both* of us?"

"It's not for *us*. Stark, this way," Monty said, stepping off to one side with Stark. "Here are the symbols I was thinking."

Monty began tracing runes into the dust on the floor.

When Monty finished, Stark released a sharp exhalation and slowly shook his head as he walked around the designs Monty had traced.

"It's possible, but it's suicide," Stark said after performing a full circuit of the symbols. "Who's going to do it?"

"Do what?" I asked warily. "What exactly do we need someone to do?"

"This design is an erasure and a tether combined in one," Stark said, staring at Monty. "If we survive this, I'd like to know where you learned this." He pointed at one of the symbols in particular. "This here is one of the lost runes. I've only seen it partially drawn. Where did *you* learn the entire symbol? Nasty piece of work, that is."

"Can you do it?" Monty said, dodging the question and holding out the ring. "Is it possible?"

"Yes," Stark said, taking the ring from Monty. "You still haven't answered who's going to do it."

"Do...what?" I said again. "What are we doing?"

"In order for this to work," Stark said, "you need to put this ring"—he held out his hand with the ring in his palm—"on the dark mage up there"—he pointed up with his other hand—"and cast an erasure on him, activating the runic catalyst."

I turned to Monty.

"How exactly are you planning to get him to wear a self-destructing ring?" I said. "Ask him politely? I don't think either of us possess *that* much diplomacy."

"There's more," Stark said. "In order to activate the catalyst, you need a blood sacrifice."

"A what?"

"Whoever places the ring on Mahnes has to sacrifice blood," Stark said. "This is why the lost runes are lost." He glanced at Monty. "They're too dangerous to be used."

"How much blood?"

"How much blood do you have?" Stark said. "It's a blood sacrifice, not a blood-sugar test. I'm going to guess plenty more than a few drops. These things don't come with exact measurements. Enough blood to get the catalyst started, I'm guessing."

"I'll do it," I said. "Out of all of us, I'm the most qualified."

"To do what? Shed blood and die? You're human like the rest of us."

"Not entirely. I'm the most qualified to shed blood and *not* die."

"The most qualified?" Stark barked. "Mahnes will tear you apart the moment you try to get close. Hell, he almost did that without getting close. Plus, you'd still have to get past those new Unbound. You'd never make it."

"We'll take that chance," Monty said. "Inscribe and imbue it, please."

"I'm going to need a moment," Stark said moving to one side. "This is complicated. That lost rune is tricky."

Monty nodded.

"We still have some time before the Unbound break through the barrier," Monty said looking up. "I wouldn't dally."

"Those Unbound, as you call them," Jarman said just above a whisper, her voice haunted. "Those were my people, my responsibilty."

"Kath, you had no way of knowing what would

happen," I said, turning to her. "The part of Mahnes is... currently being played by one psycho god who goes by Chaos."

"Doesn't matter. I should have been ready," Jarman said. "They should have never gone in like that. I don't understand. We launched the missiles; that should have taken him out. We cleared them out. How did he survive?"

"He's much stronger now with Chaos using his body," Monty said. "If we can manage to erase and tether Mahnes, Chaos will have to leave his body. He uses mages as his human hosts—specifically, dark mages."

"If he leaves, where exactly does he go?" I said. "I mean, I thought he was on an extended vacation last time. It didn't stick. Where would he go this time?"

"Last time?" Jarman said. "You've faced this madman before?"

"He was wearing a different magic user last time, but yes," I said. "This time he's upgraded to Dark Mage Batshit Edition. Monty, any ideas about where Chaos goes, or better yet, where he is?"

"I don't know," Monty said. "The fact that he prefers using dark mages is an unproven theory. What I *do* know is that if we don't stop him here and now, this will become a city of Unbound, and he won't just stop there. Millions more will die."

Stark walked over with the softly glowing blue ring in his hand. He held it out to Monty, who held it out to me.

"It's done," Stark said. "It should work. I've never worked with lost runes, but the symbol is intact. I still think it's suicide."

"Only if I die," I said, taking the ring. "I'll take the

One Ring and put it on him. This is going to hurt, but it's not going to kill me, I hope."

Stark just stared at me for a few seconds.

"How can you be so sure?" Stark said. "He's stronger than all of us combined. You're going to die—we're all going to die."

I felt the shift of energy behind us and heard the growl of my favorite hellhound. I turned and saw an exhausted Peaches, tongue lolling, slowly pad in my direction before plopping down on his side at my feet.

"Hello, boy," I said, crouching down to rub his head and belly. "Did you find him?"

<I found him. He was very far away. I'm so tired. I need to nap.>

<You did good, boy. Where is he? Where is the old bird man?>

<He's coming. He had to put on clothes. I think I scared him. He jumped and said some words I didn't understand. The dark bird lady laughed.>

A green flash filled the vaults a few seconds later, followed by plenty of cursing in a language I couldn't understand. That was the amazing thing about profanity: you didn't have to understand the language to know the intent behind the words.

"What is that?" Stark said. "Who is that?"

Dex turned around and faced us with a scowl. He was wearing a black dress shirt, black slacks, and held Nemain in one hand. His feet were bare and his expression was just this side of murderous. I took a step back, just in case he felt like swinging that lethal psycho axe mace in my direction.

"By blood, bone, and blade, nephew," Dex said, keeping

his voice low, "if you ever send that hound for me again without some kind of warning, I'll blast you into your next life." Dex turned to me and pointed with his weapon. "You need to train that hound to knock or howl or growl before just appearing. Even the Hounds of Annwn had the decency to howl their approach."

"How did he get in here?" Jarman said, looking around. "Who is that?"

"*That* is our chance to even the odds against Mahnes," I said with a small smile of relief. "Did Peaches catch you at a bad time?"

"A bad time? A bad time?" Dex growled, glaring at me. "Ach, no, boy, not at all. Mo and I were in the midst of"— he glanced at Jarman—"intimate relations when your hellhound pops into the room, nearly giving me a heart attack. You nearly lost your hellhound, and I nearly lost some of my more delicate bits. Not a bad time at all."

"Did he say hellhound?" Jarman asked. "Is that dog a hellhound? You domesticated a hellhound?"

"I wouldn't exactly say *domesticated*—he's still quite infernal. I just keep him well fed."

"Dex," I said, changing the subject of Peaches to more immediate matters. "I'm so sorry to hear Peaches interrupted you. Really, I am." I tried to keep a straight face and failed.

"I'm glad you find this amusing," Dex said, still scowling. "I've roamed this earth a long time, boy. I *will* remember and pay you back in kind. Now, what is the emergency, and there better be an emer—"

The door and barrier keeping the Unbound out began to fall with a great tearing sound followed by screeching.

We all turned at the sound and I noticed Monty subtly sweeping a foot across the runes he had traced for Stark.

"We're at Connor's?" Dex asked, looking around. "Activate the defenses upstairs."

"There is no upstairs, upstairs," I said, glancing at Jarman. "NYTF nuked the lawn to nothing."

"Runic ordnance?" Dex said, turning to Jarman, who nodded. "Are ye mad?"

"We thought we got them all," Jarman said. "We *did* get them all, except the dark mage."

"Then who are those coming to end our lives? Figments of my imagination?"

"Those were my people. That dark mage turned them into those things, those Unbound."

"Aye, lass, I'm sorry," Dex said with regret. "You can't help them now, except to put them out of their misery."

"They were my responsibility. I sent them in."

Dex looked at her, his expression hard, and nodded.

"Yes, they were. You plan on crying about it, or honoring their deaths?"

"I'll make sure they didn't die in vain," Jarman said, squaring her shoulders and drawing her gun. "They died protecting this city."

"Aye, lass. Let's not let it be for nothing," Dex said and turned to Monty. "Nephew, the plan?"

"Simon?" Monty said. "Show him."

I showed Dex the ring. He took it from my hand and examined it closely. A second later, he narrowed his eyes at Monty who conveniently looked away at that moment.

"This should work," Dex said, handing me back the ring. "If we make it out of this in one piece, there's a particular rune in the sequence we should discuss: the lost one, and how *you* found the complete symbol."

"Of course," Monty said. "Stark and I can distract the Unbound—"

"Distract the Unbound?" Stark exclaimed, raising his voice. "I'm not a fighter, I'm a craftsman. I make things. I don't get into fights."

"Today, you fight," Dex said, hefting Nemain menacingly. "Even a craftsman can wield a weapon when his life hangs in the balance."

Dex gestured and formed a silver sword, handing it to Stark hilt first, who tested the balance of the blade.

"This is exquisite," Stark said, admiring the sword. "Dwarven make."

"Aye, you know your steel," Dex said. "That there is *Neit*. He has quite a bite and will serve you well."

"Stark and I will distract and hold back the Unbound," Monty said, continuing. "Simon and Director Jarman will wait for their opening to place the ring on Mahnes. Once the ring is on, I will begin the blood ritual. Everyone who is not Simon needs to be distanced from Mahnes."

"Can he survive it?" Dex said, looking at me. "*That* blood ritual is deadly."

"If anyone can, it's him," Monty said. "If I see it going wrong, I will adjust."

Dex nodded and narrowed his eyes at Monty with a concerned look.

"I'm fine, Uncle," Monty said, catching the look. "This is the only way."

"Monty, can you protect Peaches?" I said. "I think he's going to have to sit this one out."

"Of course." Monty gestured, and a violet lattice

covered Peaches, causing him to vanish from sight. I could still sense our bond, but he was invisible. "All that remains is for my uncle to confront Mahnes and—"

"Create the opening," Dex said with a scary smile as he swung Nemain a few times. "I intend to create several. It's about time I had a proper fight."

"Is he serious?" Jarman said under her breath next to me. "He actually sounds happy."

"It's best not to try and understand him," I said. "Just be glad he's on our side."

"I don't know," she said, glancing at Dex. "He seems scarier than the dark mage upstairs. Are you sure he's mentally stable? He sounds slightly unhinged."

"I wouldn't exactly say slightly. More like completely."

Jarman stared at me as I reached into my pocket and gave her one of my remaining magazines.

"You're serious?"

"About Dex? Totally, he's insane," I said, then swtiched topics. "These are entropy rounds—"

"Entropy rounds are banned," Jarman said, looking down. Black wispy energy wafted up from the magazine. "How did you—?"

"Long story," I interrupted. "If we survive this, I'll tell you all about it. They should fit your weapon. We're trailing Dex, but not too closely. Some of the Unbound may take a swipe at you. Do *not* let them touch you. You shoot them first, understand?"

"Those were my people. They were good..."

"Not anymore," I said abruptly. "Now, all they want to do is rip your life force from your body. *You* shoot first. Let me hear it."

"I shoot first," she said as the screeching of the

Unbound filled the stairwell and the vaults. She loaded the entropy rounds into her gun with a grim determination. "I shoot first."

"You got it," I said, drawing Grim Whisper and squeezing her shoulder. "Let's do this."

TWENTY-NINE

Dex ran ahead of us with a scream that matched the sound of the Unbound headed our way. For a brief moment, I imagined facing him on a battlefield wielding Nemain.

I probably would've been one of the men running in the other direction.

The Unbound spilled into the vaults, filling the space as Dex unleashed a flurry of teleportation circles into the swarm, clearing a path to the figure in the back. Kath and I kept close to him as he carved through the Unbound.

The vaults were easily the size of several city blocks. I peered to the opposite end from where we stood and couldn't make out where they ended.

"Mahnes!" Dex screamed, his voice reverberating throughout the vaults. "Come face *me*!"

Behind us, I could see Monty and Stark dispatching Unbound as they swarmed on their location, avoiding the shredding that was Dex and his weapon. We closed in behind him, evading most of the Unbound as they converged on Monty, who had created an enormous orb of golden light.

I could feel the energy from my position and realized he was deliberately getting their attention. In front of us, I felt the presence of the dark mage as we stepped into an open area. I pulled Kath to one side and let Dex go ahead of us.

"This is where we get off," I said, keeping my voice low and moving slowly along the wall. "When we see the opening, we take it."

Dex stepped forward, a green aura of energy wrapped tight around his body. He swung Nemain and looked at Mahnes with a grin on his face.

"My quarrel is not with you, Harbinger," Chaos said. "This does not concern you. Leave now, and I will spare your life."

"Funny you should say that," Dex said. "You tried to kill those under my protection, that means I have a quarrel with you. That makes it my concern."

"Do you know whom you face?" Chaos said. "You cannot defeat me."

"Oh, I know who you are, old one," Dex said, circling around the space as Chaos matched his movements. "I don't need to defeat you, I just need to make it impossible for you to stay in that body."

"Very well, Harbinger," Chaos said, forming a sword of black energy. "I will be honored to end your life."

"You won't be the first to try," Dex said, closing the distance. "Let's see what you're made of."

Chaos unleashed a blast of black energy. Dex brought Nemain down and deflected it into a nearby wall, punching a hole into the marble, then slashed a hand down in front of him—and a swarm of green teleportation circles raced at Chaos.

Chaos backpedaled and swung his sword horizontally, slicing through the circles. Dex had used the circles as a distraction, allowing him to get close. He brought Nemain down in a strike designed to cut Chaos in half.

Chaos brought his sword up at the last moment, catching the blow inches away from his head. He aimed his free hand, covered in black energy at Dex's face.

Dex pulled down on Nemain, throwing off the blast designed to remove his head. The blast of black energy went wide, missing him as he rolled to the side, slashing at Chaos' thigh and cutting him.

Blood flowed freely from the large wound.

"First blood to you, Harbinger," Chaos said with a laugh as he disengaged, stepping back from Dex. "Well done, but you have given a dark mage access to blood."

"*Feisi*!" Dex said, gesturing. "Bloody hell!"

"Yes," Chaos said, swiping a hand on his leg and flinging the blood at Dex. The droplets became hundreds of tiny shards racing at Dex. "Bloody hell, indeed."

In one smooth move, Dex absorbed Nemain, placed his hands together in the fashion of prayer, and separated them, creating a large disc of green energy in front of his body. The blood shards crashed into the disc, as Dex reformed Nemain and charged through them, slamming into Chaos, using Nemain as a battering ram.

Chaos raised a hand in surprise as Dex collided with him, taking them both to the ground. They rolled for a few feet as Chaos unleashed blasts at Dex, who dodged and deflected them.

"This would be the opening, boy!" Dex yelled, swinging

the mace into Chaos' side with bone-crunching force. It didn't even register on Chaos' face. "It's now or never!"

"Let's go!" I said, moving fast, with Jarman in tow. She had her free hand on my back as we closed in, firing at the Unbound that were locked on us. I took half a second to look back down the vault and lock eyes with Monty, who nodded at me.

I slid next to Dex, who managed to grab one of Chaos' arms and extend it, I slid the ring over a finger and it clamped down, constricting around the finger. Chaos punched Dex in the jaw, whipping his head around. He followed up the punch with a palm to Dex's chest, blasting him with black energy that catapulted him across the floor.

Dex grinned and spit up blood as he got on all fours.

"Now it's a fight," Dex said with a growl as he stood up. "Tristan!"

The golden orb behind us exploded with light as Chaos looked down at his hand in surprise.

"You think this trinket is going to stop me? You stupid, foolish children," Chaos said, forming his sword again. "I am ever present. I am infinite. I am entropy. I am everlasting. You will never be able to stand before me."

Chaos raised his sword to remove his hand. Before Dex or I could react, Jarman lunged forward and grabbed his arm, deflecting the blow with her body.

"Kath, no!" I yelled as a beam of golden light shot past me and into Chaos, beginning the blood ritual and erasure. "Nonono...what did you do?"

Chaos dropped his sword as he screamed, grabbing Jarman by the throat. Blood flowed from her eyes, ears, and nose. She bled freely for what seemed an eternity as

Chaos writhed in agony, falling to his knees and dragging her to the floor as he lost consciousness.

When he finally let her go, she collapsed to the floor next to him, pale and barely conscious. Monty and Stark ran over as Dex looked over Mahnes' body.

"Did we...did we get him?" Jarman asked weakly. "Tell me we got him."

"We got him...you got him," I said, holding her cold hand. "*You* did it."

She smiled.

"Good. They didn't die for nothing," she said, looking at me and fading fast. "Make sure you tell Angel I saved his city. You tell him I saved his ass."

"Hold on, Jarman. Stay with me," I said, looking from Monty to Dex with pleading eyes. They both shook their heads slowly. I looked back down at Jarman. "I'll make sure he knows."

"Thank you," Jarman said. "Make sure the officers are remembered as people, not those monsters."

"I will."

"Good. That's good," she said with one last sigh as her lifeless eyes looked past me.

Next to her, Mahnes groaned and I aimed Grim Whisper at his head.

Dex put a hand on my arm and shook his head.

"Are you kidding me? After everything he's done? A bullet in his head is mercy."

"Not your place, boy," Dex said, his voice grim. "He let himself be used by one of the old ones... This is above your pay grade."

"Who, then?" I said, raising my voice. "Are you going to do it? Because if you're not going to do it, then I am."

"This one is above mine, too," Dex said, stepping back. "Holster your weapon, lad. Wouldn't want you to get hurt."

"Who, then?" I demanded again, holstering Grim Whisper. "Who is going to make sure this piece of scum meets justice?"

"I will," a voice said behind me. "This one is mine."

It was Badb Catha.

I looked at Mahnes, who had regained consciousness, and shook my head. He sneered in my direction. The sneer quickly transformed to a look of terror as Badb stepped close.

Everyone's a badass until they face pain and death.

"You're going to wish they'd let me shoot you," I said, backing up and stepping out of her way. "I hope whatever she does to you takes a long time and hurts more than anything has ever hurt you."

"He *will* suffer before the end," Badb said and looked down at Jarman. "This one died a warrior and fell in battle. Make sure she is properly honored."

"I—we will," I said, giving her more space as a cloud of dark energy began pouring out of her. The black energy engulfed Mahnes, hiding him from sight. "Where is Chaos?"

"The old one roams this plane still, looking for another host," Badb said, glancing down at where I last saw Mahnes. "Do not let down your guard. He seeks you still, Marked of Kali."

"Wonderful," I said under my breath. "I'm really going to need a power upgrade."

Badb Catha turned to Dex, who bravely stood his ground. She stepped close to him and ran a finger along his jaw. Dex remained completely still.

"The smell of battle still lingers on your skin," she said huskily. "We will continue our conversation when you return."

Dex could only nod once as the energy around Badb Catha expanded, disappearing her from view. When she was gone, Dex let out a long sigh and I just stared at him.

"You are one crazy old man," I said as he grinned. "Have you grown tired of living?"

"Ach, lad, life is meant to be lived," Dex said. "The only way to do that is to be near death on a regular basis."

"No," I said, shaking my head. "The only way to do that is to be on a beach, drinking something cold and potent. Not dancing with death on a regular basis."

"Chaos is still out there," Dex said. "You may get that dance yet."

"Can I at least go home and take a shower first?" I protested. "Maybe drink a enormous, potentially lethal jug of Deathwish?"

Dex smiled and then grew serious as he looked at Monty and me.

"You're right about one thing," he said. "You two need to upgrade. There is a mage. He's old, cranky and antisocial—"

"Oh, so he's like most typical mages?"

"Worse, but he will help you both," Dex said. "Tell him I sent you and then show him the lost rune, nephew. He'll either agree or try to kill you both. Hard to tell with him. Really depends on the day and his mood."

"This mage have a name?"

"York," Dex said. "He was once in the Golden Circle; solid mage, but an absolute nutter regarding most everything else. Only mage I recall fighting me to a draw. I'll come by later and leave you his address."

"Where exactly does this nutter live?" I said. "Just for the sake of logistics."

"That might complicate things a bit," Dex said, rubbing his chin. "Last I recall, he was in London. I'm pretty sure he's still there. In any case, you need to see him before Chaos finds you...again. It's settled."

Stark handed Neit back to Dex who reabsorbed it.

"It was an amazing weapon," Stark said. "Thank you for allowing me to use it."

"My pleasure," Dex said. "Today, you were a warrior."

"Thank you. Tristan?" Stark said. "May I have it, please?"

"Of course," Monty said, reaching into his pocket and giving Stark the ring he had entrusted him with. "Are you sure you want to do this? We can help."

"Thank you, but no. I appreciate it, but I think I should do this alone," Stark said, putting on the ring. "I have to know. At the very least, they deserve to be put to rest properly. Thank you for everything. I hope one day I can repay you."

I nodded to Stark. I didn't dislike the shop teacher. I understood why he'd done what he had, but at the end of the day, he had risked my and my family's lives to save his own. Just because I understood it, didn't mean I liked it.

He nodded back, touched parts of the ring in sequence, and vanished with a flash of red light.

"What was that?" I said, blinking against the blinding after-effects. "Some kind of teleport?"

"That ring is a blood tether," Monty said. "He'll be able to locate his family, wherever they may be."

"Alive?"

"Alive or not," Monty said. "That tether will take him to them. I hope he finds them."

"I hope it's alive."

"As do I," Monty said, looking down at Jarman. "We need to tend to her."

"She stays here," Dex said, his voice firm. "Anyone wants to argue that point, you send them to me. I'll put her next to my brother. She's earned it."

Dex gestured and Jarman's body slowly faded from sight as Monty nodded.

"That would be fitting," he said. "Simon, collect your creature. It seems we need to pack for a trip."

I reached out through my bond and sensed where Peaches lay.

<Let's go home, boy. Hello?>

Nothing.

<Monty is going to make you those five sausages he promised.>

My hellhound materialized next to me, bumping into my side with a low rumble, nearly launching me across the floor.

<Meat! What took so long? I took a short nap. It was so good.>

<Naps are the best, I agree.>

<Naps after meat are even better.>

For once I couldn't argue with my hellhound.

"Let's go home," I said, heading to the stairs. "I'm exhausted and in need of sleep. About a week's worth."

"An excellent idea," Monty said, looking at Dex. "Perhaps some food first. Care to join us, Uncle?"

"And keep Mo waiting? I'm not *that* suicidal," he said with a mischievous grin. "I'll catch up with you both later. Thank you for the fight."

He gestured and disappeared with a green flash.

"Your uncle is one strange mage," I said as I walked past the destruction around us. "It's going to take some work to fix this place."

"I'll make sure it's handled," Monty said. "I could use a strong cuppa."

"Ezra's is probably open," I said. "I'll even brave the stink eyes for one of his pastrami sandwiches and egg creams."

"I think your creature is starting to rub off on you."

"Hey, haven't you heard? Meat is life."

Peaches chuffed and rumbled next to me.

"Seems I'm outvoted," Monty said with a small smile. "Ezra's it is."

"Afterwards, we'll go see how Angel is doing," I said. "I need to tell him about Jarman. He'll want to pay his respects."

Monty nodded.

"He deserves to know," Monty said. "I can arrange for him to visit here when he recovers."

We left the cemetery behind and stepped into the brightening sky of a new day. We won, but the cost, the cost was steep. Chaos was still out there, somewhere, but right now, in this moment, I'd take the victory of seeing another morning.

THE END

AUTHOR NOTES

Thank you for reading this story and jumping into the world of Monty & Strong with me.

Disclaimer: The Author Notes are written at the very end of the writing process. This section is not seen by the ART or my amazing Jeditor—Audrey. Any typos or errors following this disclaimer are mine and mine alone.

Book 14...If you've read this far, in this book and the series, thank you and WOW. I never thought we'd get this far, but Monty & Strong show no signs of letting me go. DIVINE INTERVENTION and the books following it will ramp up the danger and pace considerably.

I want to give a huge shout out to the most amazing readers on the planet, my MoB Family! I write these stories for you and your reading the stories continues to spur me on to keep writing these fantastic stories.

Like I said at the end of REQUIEM, the next few books will be full of upheaval, danger, death, and explosions. Some of the characters will mature and grow, becoming even more important and others...well, others will elegantly, gracefully, and gloriously bow out of the M&S World as their lives come to an end.

I promise to make it awesome and maybe shed a tear or two.

Simon has literally become a marked target and the next books will continue to weave this thread into the stories until he gets strong enough to scare those who would attempt to eliminate him...or he dies. Whichever comes first.

It's only August, which means we have a good four months before this year is history. The time has flown. The next projects slated for this year are SEPIA BLUE-DEMON, NOCTURNE MELODY(Night Warden book 3), STORM BLOOD(M&S 15), and BANGERS & MASH. There may be some other surprises stashed in there somewhere, but I can't share them just yet, they wouldn't be surprises otherwise.

I sometimes take a moment and read my past work, usually for research or to make sure the continuity is right and I am awed at some of the words I have written. I can only thank my incredible readers and phenomenal ART for the greatness that appears in my stories. You truly do take a good story and make it a great one...thank you.

There are still plenty of short story trilogies that need to be wrapped up. I will be fitting them in as I do my best to complete the full novels. Many times what I call a short story, becomes feral and transforms into a novella. I do try to wrangle it back into a reasonable word count, but I have found that most of my 'short stories' are really novellas in disguise.

I've made peace with it.

There are quite a few novellas scheduled for next year,

some of them I'm very excited to write others...I'm excited and a little scared to give life to. The fear being that they will overtake pretty much EVERYTHING lol.

I'll still write them, though, because as Dex says: You have to live life and take those risks.

Once again, I wanted to share what an incredible honor and pleasure it is to be able to write these stories for you, my amazing readers. On the days when it's more work than play (there are a few), knowing that I'm writing this story for you helps me get through the rough patches when I want to just a fling a asteroid at the planet and call it a day.

There are always a few days when I really want to fling an asteroid, but on those days, I fill my mug with Deathwish, take a long pull and an even longer breath, play some Destiny, and then incorporate the old discipline of Sitzfleisch—butt in chair until it gets done.

Thank you again for taking the time to read this story. I wrote it for you and I hope you enjoyed spending some time with Monty & Simon as they confronted an old god who has come back to finish what he started way back in TOMBYARDS & BUTTERFLIES. Chaos isn't gone, and the threat he poses will grow with each book coming. Simon will continue to grow, maybe even getting a hang of the dawnward, maybe. There is no shortage of mages willing to give him a few lessons on the painful execution of certain casts, starting with a particularly unstable mage located in London, named, York.

Whether or not Monty & Simon survive their second trip to London remains to be seen. They will have to brave many dangers just to get there, once there, Simon's mark and Monty's past will make their lives challenging to say the least.

It promises to be a particularly volatile trip, but then again, that defines the Montague & Strong Detective Agency. Right now the future is uncertain, what I do know, is that Simon will always do his best, while striving to be a worthy friend to Monty and a never ending source of meat to his ever-ravenous hellhound and bondmate, Peaches—who we all love.

As long as you keep reading, I'll keep writing.

If you enjoyed this story—please leave a review. It's really important and helps the book (and me).

Thank you again for jumping into this story with me!

SPECIAL MENTIONS

To Dolly: my rock, anchor, and inspiration. Thank you...always.

Larry & Tammy—The WOUF: Because even when you aren't there...you're there.

Tammy: because nothing makes your eyes cross more than a decaf mocha diet whip frappe with two pumps of entitlement.

Kathy (Kath) Jarman: Welcome to being a Redshirt! Your death was indeed glorious and worthy of a M&S story.

Jo Dungey: For Simon's Redshirt observation/introduction.

Dolly Sanchez: For glowgre.

Orlando A. Sanchez
www.orlandoasanchez.com

Orlando has been writing ever since his teens when he was immersed in creating scenarios for playing Dungeons and Dragons with his friends every weekend.

The worlds of his books are urban settings with a twist of the paranormal lurking just behind the scenes and with generous doses of magic, martial arts, and mayhem.

He currently resides in Queens, NY with his wife and children.

More books by Orlando A. Sanchez

The Warriors of the Way

The Karashihan*•The Spiritual Warriors•The Ascendants•The Fallen Warrior•The Warrior Ascendant•The Master Warrior

The Assassin's Apprentice
The Birth of Death

Gideon Shepherd Thrillers
Sheepdog

DAMNED
Aftermath

RULE OF THE COUNCIL
Blood Ascension•Blood Betrayal•Blood Rule

NYXIA WHITE
They Bite•They Rend•They Kill

IKER THE CLEANER
Iker the Unseen

*Books denoted with an asterisk are **FREE** via my website—www.orlandoasanchez.com

ART SHREDDERS

I want to take a moment to extend a special thanks to the ART SHREDDERS.

No book is the work of one person. I am fortunate enough to have an amazing team of advance readers and shredders.

Thank you for giving of your time and keen eyes to provide notes, insights, answers to the questions, and corrections (dealing wonderfully with my extreme dreaded comma allergy). You help make every book and story go from good to great. Each and every one of you helped make this book fantastic, and I couldn't do this without each of you.

THANK YOU

ART SHREDDERS

Amber, Anne Morando, Audrey Cienki
Bethany Showell, Beverly Collie

Cam Skaggs, Carrie Anne O'Leary, Cat, Chris Christman II, Colleen Taylor

Darren Musson, Dawn McQueen Mortimer, Denise King, Desmond, Diana Gray, Diane Craig, Diane Kassmann, Dolly Sanchez, Donna Young Hatridge

Hal Bass, Helen Gibson

Jasmine Breeden, Jasmine Davis, Jeanette Auer, Jen Cooper, John Fauver, Joy Kiili, Julie Peckett

Karen Hollyhead

Larry Diaz Tushman

Malcolm Robertson, Marcia Campbell, Maryelaine Eckerle-Foster, Melissa Miller

Nick Church

Paige Guido, Penny Campbell-Myhill

RC Battels, Rene Corrie

Sara Mason Branson, Sean Trout, Shannon Owens Bainbridge, Sondra Massey, Stacey Stein, Stephanie Claypoole, Susie Johnson

Tami Cowles, Tanya Anderson, Ted Camer, Terri Adkisson, Thomas Ryan

Vikki Brannagan

Wendy Schindler

ACKNOWLEDEGEMENTS

With each book, I realize that every time I learn something about this craft, it highlights so many things I still have to learn. Each book, each creative expression, has a large group of people behind it.

This book is no different.

Even though you see one name on the cover, it is with the knowledge that I am standing on the shoulders of the literary giants that informed my youth, and am supported by my generous readers who give of their time to jump into the adventures of my overactive imagination.

I would like to take a moment to express my most sincere thanks:

To Dolly: My wife and greatest support. You make all this possible each and every day. You keep me grounded when I get lost in the forest of ideas. Thank you for asking the right questions when needed, and listening intently when I go off on tangents. Thank you for who you are and the space you create—I love you.

To my Tribe: You are the reason I have stories to tell. You cannot possibly fathom how much and how deeply I love you all.

To Lee: Because you were the first audience I ever had. I love you, sis.

To the Logsdon Family: The words *thank you* are insufficient to describe the gratitude in my heart for each of you. JL, your support always demands I bring my best, my A-game, and produce the best story I can. Both you and Lorelei (my Uber Jeditor) and now, Audrey, are the reason I am where I am today. My thank you for the notes, challenges, corrections, advice, and laughter. Your patience is truly infinite. *Arigatogozaimasu.*

To The Montague & Strong Case Files Group—AKA The MoB (Mages of Badassery): When I wrote T&B there were fifty-five members in The MoB. As of this release, there are over one thousand four hundred members in the MoB. I am honored to be able to call you my MoB Family. Thank you for being part of this group and M&S.

You make this possible. **THANK YOU.**

To the ever-vigilant PACK: You help make the MoB... the MoB. Keeping it a safe place for us to share and just...

be. Thank you for your selfless vigilance. You truly are the Sentries of Sanity.

Chris Christman II: A real-life technomancer who makes the **MoBTV LIVEvents +Kaffeeklatsch** on YouTube amazing. Thank you for your tireless work and wisdom. Everything is connected...you totally rock!

To the WTA—The Incorrigibles: JL, Ben Z. Eric QK., S.S., and Noah.

They sound like a bunch of badass misfits, because they are. My exposure to the deranged and deviant brain trust you all represent helped me be the author I am today. I have officially gone to the *dark side* thanks to all of you. I humbly give you my thanks, and...it's all your fault.

To my fellow Indie Authors, specifically the tribe at 20books to 50k: Thank you for creating a space where authors can feel listened to, and encouraged to continue on this path. A rising tide lifts all the ships indeed.

To The English Advisory: Aaron, Penny, Carrie, Davina, and all of the UK MoB. For all things English...thank you.

To DEATH WISH COFFEE: This book (and every book I write) has been fueled by generous amounts of the only coffee on the planet (and in space) strong enough to power my very twisted imagination. Is there any other coffee that can compare? I think not. DEATHWISH —thank you!

To Deranged Doctor Design: Kim, Darja, Tanja, Jovana, and Milo (Designer Extraordinaire).

If you've seen the covers of my books and been amazed, you can thank the very talented and gifted creative team at DDD. They take the rough ideas I give them, and produce incredible covers that continue to surprise and amaze me. Each time, I find myself striving to write a story worthy of the covers they produce. DDD, you embody professionalism and creativity. Thank you for the great service and spectacular covers. **YOU GUYS RULE!**

To you, the reader: I was always taught to save the best for last. I write these stories for **you**. Thank you for jumping down the rabbit holes of *what if?* with me. You are the reason I write the stories I do.

You keep reading...I'll keep writing.

Thank you for your support and encouragement.

CONTACT ME

I really do appreciate your feedback. You can let me know what you thought of the story by emailing me at:
orlando@orlandoasanchez.com

To get **FREE** stories please visit my page at:
www.orlandoasanchez.com

For more information on the M&S World...come join the MoB Family on Facebook!
You can find us at:
Montague & Strong Case Files

Visit our online M&S World Swag Store located at:
Emandes

If you enjoyed the book, **please leave a review**. Reviews help the book, and also help other readers find good stories to read.
THANK YOU!

Thanks for Reading

If you enjoyed this book, would you **please leave a review** at the site you purchased it from? It doesn't have to be a book report... just a line or two would be fantastic and it would really help us out!

Made in the USA
Middletown, DE
11 May 2022